THE GROOM'S DAUGHTER

BY
NATALIE FOX

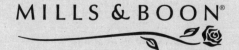
MILLS & BOON®

First published in Great Britain 1998
Harlequin Mills & Boon Limited,
Eton House, 18-24 Paradise Road, Richmond, Surrey TW9 1SR

© Natalie Fox 1998

ISBN 0 263 80715 0

Set in Times Roman 10½ on 11¼ pt.
01-9803-57244 C1

Printed and bound in Great Britain
by Mackays of Chatham PLC, Chatham

'I'm not who you think I am.'

Nina continued, 'You came to get a Nina Parker and, yes, that is my name. But you have made some sort of ghastly mistake.'

Lorenzo shook his head. 'No, Nina, you made the mistake in coming to Sicily to look for your lover. You won't stop this wedding. It goes ahead without you. Now, do as you are told and bathe, and then we will talk and negotiate.'

This wasn't happening! According to Lorenzo, she had come to Sicily to stop her lover's wedding. But she *had* no lover. And what sort of negotiations was he talking about?

He'd made a mistake but he wasn't the sort of man to admit it. Nina *had* to convince him he'd got the wrong person!

Natalie Fox was born and brought up in London and has a daughter, two sons and two grandchildren. Her husband, Ian, is a retired advertising executive, and they now live in a tiny Welsh village. Natalie is passionate about her cats—two strays brought back from Spain where she lived for five years—and equally passionate about gardening and writing romance. Natalie says she took up writing because she absolutely *hates* going out to work!

Recent titles by the same author:

MAN TROUBLE!
A MARRIAGE IN THE MAKING

CHAPTER ONE

'YOU are wrong, *signora*!' Nina protested fiercely, lifting her hands to ward off the furious woman. 'I would not—'

'You, out, you bad girl,' Silvestra Locasto screamed, pushing so forcefully Nina stumbled against the olive tree in the cobbled courtyard of the Locastos' townhouse, grazing her arm on the rough bark.

The two Sicilian housemaids were following close behind, dragging Nina's belongings with them, trying to stifle their laughter for fear of the mistress turning her fury on them. The two Locasto children, who until half an hour ago had been under Nina's care, made no attempt to control their amusement; they laughed openly, pointed their fat fingers and jeered.

Putting aside this latest humiliation, Nina was almost glad it had come to this—being forcibly evicted from this horrible house. She had hated it from day one. Was it only two weeks ago? It had felt like a long-term prison sentence, with hard labour thrown in and not the faintest chance of parole. She had stuck at it, though; considering her dire financial circumstances, she'd had no choice but to grin and bear it.

Now she was out of it. Hardly with her pride and honour intact, but the indignity was almost worth suffering to be free of those hideous spoilt brats, their ghastly mother, who was nothing more than a jumped-up fishwife, and Emilio Locasto… Oh, God, she hadn't known such men still existed. Sweaty, slimy and amazingly convinced his sole reason for being put on this earth was for women's benefit and joy.

5

Nina hugged her grazed arm and suppressed a shudder at the thought of that man trying to touch her, trying to tempt her with sickening innuendos. The gall of him, the horror of him, *and* his awful children, who had taken such pleasure in driving her to distraction, and now this, the fury of a jealous wife who obviously had a serious sight problem if she believed another woman might find her husband attractive.

Silvestra grasped Nina's long flaxen hair and shoved her towards the wrought-iron gates that opened out into the street.

'You try take my husband but he no want skinny,' Silvestra screamed. 'You out! You out in the street where you belong.'

The maids gleefully swung the gates open for her and Silvestra took great pride in jerking Nina towards the opening, but before she thrust her out she swung her around to face her.

'You ask for money. I no pay a whore,' she shouted furiously for all to hear. And there were plenty to hear, Nina realised with another wash of humiliation flooding her. It seemed every housewife in the street was watching her eviction from the tall, narrow townhouse of the supposedly respected Locasto family. 'You act like whore, you do business out here.'

Nina rebelled at this last insult. She'd had nothing but stress and misery thrown at her since arriving in Sicily to look for her father—a father she didn't know, a father she burned to know. The whole trip was turning into a fiasco, and if she hadn't been so stubborn she would have turned tail and fled, returned to England and admitted the whole idea had been a naive attempt to find her roots. But a defeatist she wasn't.

Furiously Nina tore herself out of the grip of the woman, grey eyes wide with determination not to take any more insults and indignities. But almost as soon as the rebellion fired it flickered uncertainly. What was she going to do? Wrestle this woman in the gutter with an audience of thousands rooting for their own? Her shoulders sagged in defeat, but Silvestra Locasto wasn't finished with her audience or her victim yet. She puffed herself up like some bird of prey ready to swoop, ready to give her admiring audience the final triumphant act. And Nina wasn't at all prepared for it as the woman's hand came up and lashed across the side of her face. She reeled back with shock, and was even more horrified to hear cries of encouragement from the other women.

Real fear looped down her spine then. She was an alien, a foreigner, who, according to Signora Locasto, was a husband-stealer. She wouldn't stand a chance against the collected wrath of these Sicilian women. But she had her pride, oh, boy, yes, she did have some spirit left—inherited from the father she had come to seek. After all, wasn't she part Sicilian herself? She thinned her pale lips meaningfully.

'You pay me what you owe me, *signora*,' she seethed. 'If you don't pay me I'll tell the street what a bad employer you are.'

Hands on hips, the woman threw her head back and laughed out loud. Then she humiliated Nina further by swinging her around so she was facing the street and then heaving her great bulk at Nina's slight form, sending her staggering out into the hot, dusty road.

Try as she might, feet skidding for support in worn espadrilles, Nina lurched forward, lost her balance and sprawled inelegantly into the gutter. Shaken and winded, her head reeled dizzily as her fingers clawed at debris collected in the gutter.

More indignity followed as missiles suddenly started hurling down on her. Overripe tomatoes splattered around her; water, bucketed out from a window above, narrowly missed her but splashed her face and hair. Then she heard her backpack thud next to her, and the clunk of the glass bead necklace she had hung on her mirror to cheer that ghastly bare room, jammed down in the base-ment next to the laundry room. She heard a collected roar of approval from the women watching the humilia-tion of a supposed husband-snatcher, and then the clang-ing of the wrought-iron gates behind her.

It was a relief to hear those gates clang shut and the bolts driven purposefully home. The torture and the hu-miliation and the misery were finally over. She had never been so lonely, unhappy and homesick in the weeks she had worked for them—no, *slaved* for them. And now it was all behind her.

Nina took deep breaths of relief and in a moment of absurd black humour, urged on by self-preservation, she imagined a film director shouting, 'Cut!' This was a scene out of a surreal Italian film, surely?

Slowly her head cleared and she blinked open her eyes, suddenly aware of the sounds around her changing as she lay sprawled in the dust, gathering her breath. There was a new sound—the silky purr of a car engine, the click of a car door opening only feet from where she lay.

The laughter of the women onlookers faded and was replaced by a low murmur of warning to each other. Doors banged shut in the narrow street, wooden shutters on the windows slammed and bolted. Even the tiny yel-low canaries that hung caged from the balconies stopped chirruping.

The only sound now was the purr of the still running car engine. Slowly Nina lifted her head, her heart ham-mering in anticipation of what had brought about this eerie silence. The first thing she saw in the heat haze shimmering off the street was a pair of hand-stitched, highly polished crocodile shoes. A curious shade of light brown, not at all the colour she imagined a crocodile to be.

I'm hallucinating, Nina thought dizzily. She lifted her head slightly, moved her grey eyes upwards, expecting the hot sun to blind her but mercifully finding she was lying in the shadow of a giant. Long white-linen-clad legs led to more white linen. An immaculate suit jacket, Armani, without a doubt, gaped open to reveal the white silk of an open-necked shirt. Powerful arms were crossed over a wide chest; a very dark head with black, neatly tamed curls was bent towards her in hardened surveillance.

Silence heaped on more silence as time seemed to stand still. The giant didn't speak, just stood, legs apart, gazing down at her. Nina wasn't in a position to scrutinise his features thoroughly, she was simply relieved that he, whoever he might be, had arrived on the scene to silence the taunts. She was relieved, too, that he didn't wear the uniform of the *carabinieri*. After all this she didn't relish the idea of being thrown into prison when she explained she had been working for the Locastos without a work permit.

Nina made a brave attempt to struggle to her feet, but what with the heat and the brutality of her eviction she felt about as strong as a fledgling bird that had tumbled unceremoniously from its nest on its first attempt at freedom. She managed the kerb, though, sat on it, bare brown legs apart, and brushed at her scuffed knees, only thankful she was wearing shorts and not a skimpy skirt that might be up around her waist now, stripping her of the last of her dignity.

'Are you all right?' the Armani suit asked, his voice deep and resonant, his Italian accent slight.

Nina lifted her head and narrowed her grey eyes at the stranger. If she had been anywhere else but sitting awkwardly trying to get her equilibrium together, she

might have appreciated more fully that he was a strikingly good-looking guy. She was certainly alert enough
to register those looks, though. So she wasn't concussed
and, apart from the indignity, she was unscathed.

'I've felt better,' she quipped. 'Looked better, too,'
she added ruefully, brushing a few sticky tomato pips
from her upper arm.

A strong brown hand came towards her and Nina
gratefully took it, and the stranger, with very little effort,
hauled her to her feet.

'Thanks,' she responded, and managed a faint smile.
'You're the first gentleman I've come across in this part
of Palermo.' She lifted her head to look at him properly.

Now she could fully appreciate his sultry black eyes,
his fine-chiselled bone structure. His full mouth was
thinned censoriously, though, and she wondered how
much he had seen and heard of her ungainly eviction.
His taut olive skin was typical of the Sicilians, but he
also had an added sophistication. His thick black hair
was glossy and spiralled into curls most women would
envy, Nina amongst them.

Self-consciously, Nina smoothed her own hair, found
some more tomato pips and covered them with her fingers. Gosh, she must look dreadful, and he was so smart
and suave. She eyed him with curiosity, then flicked her
eyes to his car, and her generous mouth parted slightly
with shock. It was more a stretch limo than a mere car.
It was pure white with blackened windows, and the engine was still throbbing expensively.

'So, who are you, the local debt collector?' she asked
rather flippantly, recovering now and over the shock of
him and the car, which both looked totally out of place
in a narrow street of downtown Palermo.

Silence. He didn't say a word at her weak attempt at
humour. His sultry eyes narrowed quizzically but that
was all. Nina's heart suddenly tightened. What a dumb

thing to say to a stranger who had a car like that! Though she had only been in Sicily a few weeks it was long enough to soak up the atmosphere and the gossip. 'Mafioso' was the word that came to mind.

Her eyes widened and her hand dropped from her tousled hair to clench at her side. 'Um, er, thank you very much for helping me up,' she croaked. 'I'll be on my way now. *Molte grazie. Ciao!*'

She bent to snatch up her backpack, wanting to run like the wind. After all she had been through: having her money stolen from the hostel in the first week here in Palermo, finding work with the Locastos only to find she was working for the family from hell, and now her un-dignified eviction without being paid... Things couldn't get any worse!

The backpack was lifted from the ground a second before she reached it herself. Without a word the stranger turned around and, before Nina could protest, he flung it through the open passenger door of the limo.

He bent and picked up her necklace, a paperback book, a couple of sable-tipped paintbrushes and a tub of moisturising cream and flung them into the limo, too.

'No, not that!' she cried as he went to pick up a faded yellow headband that a child must have lost in the road. 'That's not mine.'

Her head spun with what she had just said. Anyone would think she had every intention of climbing into that luxurious looking car after her backpack and going off with him. Which was *his* intention, she realised with a faint heart, because he was nodding his dark head in the direction of the interior.

Nina backed off. 'No, honestly,' she protested, grimy hands held up to stress her point. 'I'm perfectly all right now. My...my boyfriend is waiting for me. Just around the corner in the *Piazzo... Piazza,*' she corrected, feeling her face growing hot and flushed at the lie she had told. If only there were a boyfriend!

He didn't believe her. His dark brows rose slightly but he didn't say a word. He simply nodded towards the open car door again.

Common sense told her not to get in, and her distress wasn't a reason to let down her reserve. And where could he take her anyway? If he was being a gentleman and helping a young lady in distress he would surely offer to take her somewhere, but where? The hostel she had been staying at before the Locasto fiasco wanted lire up front and she scarcely had enough money left for the froth on the top of a cup of cappuccino!

Her dire situation really hit her then. She was broke, horribly so. She'd had no luck whatsoever in tracing her father, and even if she wanted to give up and go home she couldn't. She was standing in a seedy part of the city, lire-less, homeless, and face to face with a...a gangster?

Her despair must have shown on her stricken face because the stranger suddenly stepped forward and very gently—that was a surprise—took her arm and led her to the car. He spoke then, very softly, very reassuringly.

'Don't be afraid. I mean you no harm, but you have had a shock and you look in need of a bath. This isn't a very nice area for a young English lady so allow me to offer my help.'

She must look ghastly for him to suggest a bath, she thought dejectedly. Some poor little waif—stupid, too, for getting herself into such a ridiculous position. Had he seen her undignified eviction from Casa Locasto? Had he heard the screams of abuse and the accusations from the *signora*?

'How...how do you know I'm English?' she asked hesitantly as, at the door of his limo, he let her go.

He nodded his head at her backpack on the seat and

a very small smile softened his dark features, a smile that had Nina wavering between sense and insensibility. She had sewn a Union Jack onto the back of the bag, thinking it might get her more lifts as she'd hitchhiked through France and down through Italy to Sicily. It had, as it happened. She'd met some lovely travellers, British as well as other Europeans. It had boded so well for her intentions at first. But since arriving here—nothing but trouble.

In spite of the small smile the dark stranger offered Nina didn't allow her reserve to slip altogether. In fact all her senses were suddenly beginning to brim up to full alert. She might still be in shock, and he might have a charming smile, but after what she had been through lately she wasn't about to land herself in another uncompromising position she couldn't get out of. After all, a guy who drove a limo with blackened windows must have something to hide, she reasoned.

'Are you going to get in or would you rather I left you here to the mercy of the street women?' he suggested smoothly. 'From what I have just seen and heard I wouldn't fancy your chances walking the streets alone.'

Her heart sank. He *had* seen and heard. He hadn't joined in the taunts, though, he had simply stopped to offer his help. But perhaps he thought her an easy pickup, believing, as Signora Locasto had said, that she ought to be plying her trade on the streets.

Nina lifted her chin defensively. She knew the truth and that was all that mattered, but as she lifted her face to defy him she caught sight of herself in the wing mirror of the suspect limo. She looked ghastly, dishevelled, very small and insignificant. Her hair was matted with tomato, her face reddened on one side where that dreadful woman had hit her. By no stretch of the imagination could she be taken for a woman of the night. Men would have to be pretty hard up to make her an offer she couldn't refuse!

This man standing in front of her, for instance. Uncertainly her eyes flicked back to the stranger. He looked the sort to have a harem of gorgeous women, *or* a stunningly beautiful wife.

'Thanks, but no, thanks,' she told him firmly, after making the decision not to get involved. And from somewhere she summoned the strength to reach into the car and snatch at her belongings. But as her fingers clawed at the straps of her backpack she felt pressure from behind.

Two very firm hands gripped her waist and her feet were suddenly off the ground. She was plopped into the passenger seat as effortlessly as if she were a bag of dirty washing about to be dropped off at the laundry. The door was slammed behind her and her ears popped as if she had been enclosed in a vacuum. Momentarily shocked though she was, she was quick to get her senses together. Clutching her pack protectively to her chest, she lurched across the seat and aimed for the driver's side, intending to scramble out of the other door, only to come face up against a hard wall of muscle.

Her breath caught in her throat. 'What on earth do you think you are doing?' she exclaimed as she lurched back from him. And how on earth had he got into the driver's seat at the speed of light?

'Acting far more sensibly than you at the moment,' he told her drily.

Nina fell back against cool white leather and caught her breath. Remarkably her first thought, naive as it was, even to herself, was that you could see out of these dark windows from the inside. Sadly not the other way around. She could press her face hard up against the window, pummel her fists at them for outside help and no one would see her.

But all was not lost. They were moving now, gliding very slowly along the narrow shadowy street. So slowly that she could easily have time to open the door and roll herself out onto the narrow pavement without coming to too much harm. She wrenched at the door but it didn't give under her touch. It was locked. Her heart sank.

Out of the corner of her eye she saw a muscle at the edge of his mouth tighten. No other giveaway on his hard, implacable face, but enough for her to know he was displeased.

So what? she thought defiantly. Did he think she was some dizzy blonde with as much sense as a...dizzy blonde? Her strength collapsed inside her. From what he knew of her so far she must have come across as some dimwit. Here she was in a less than salubrious part of town after being evicted into the street by a woman screaming abuse at her for trying to take her husband. To the stranger it could all be true.

She gulped. 'Er, where are you taking me?' she asked tentatively.

'To the *piazza*,' he answered, as if she should know. 'I shall safely deliver you to your boyfriend and go on my way,' he finalised.

And that was it. Nina squirmed in her seat, uncomfortably reasoning that she was mildly disappointed and the feeling was definitely an odd one. So he had believed her defensive lie and was about to act on it—and she was *disappointed*?

And not for the reason that there would be no boyfriend there waiting for her. She lifted her hand to move her damp, dishevelled hair from her brow. Enclosed in this cool, air-conditioned limo with this suave stranger, she was beginning to feel very odd indeed.

But after fighting off the evil Emilio for two weeks now she should be even more wary of men. But this one was different. She was aware of him rather than wary of him, though that was a contradiction. She had *tried* to refuse his offer of help. And, absurdly, was now a trifle disappointed that it wasn't going any further than the wretched *piazza*. Perhaps she was a little concussed after all.

'Thank you,' she mumbled, and sat very still beside him, eyes facing ahead rather than dare take a sideways peek at him.

At last she took a sidelong look at his face. Implacably he stared ahead through the windscreen, giving nothing of himself away. He was like stone, beautiful stone, sculptured stone, and curiously Nina's heart clenched.

He turned suddenly, so quickly she had no time to take evasive action herself and look away. She went scarlet, though, embarrassed at being caught looking at him. He took a silk handkerchief from his top pocket and thrust it at her before averting his eyes back to the street. He turned smoothly into another narrow street before speaking.

'Clean yourself up,' he ordered without emotion.

Nina obeyed, lifting the warm silk from her lap where it had landed and rubbing it across her hot, stinging face. Her head swam with the lemony fragrance from it. It was too good to rub over the scuffs on her knees and mop up the tiny trickle of blood on her arm from her brush with the olive tree so she clutched the silk in her hands, twisting the ends between her fingers, not expecting him to demand it back.

She stared bleakly ahead, knowing the next turn would bring them into the *piazza*. And then what? She would leap out, effuse her thanks and scuttle off down some back alley once he was gone. And to where? Her heart was heavy at the thought. She had nowhere to go.

A few weeks back she would have taken up the challenge with zeal but she was weakening now. You could only take so much bad luck. Perhaps she should have listened to Jonathan's pleas for her not to go on this wild-goose chase of hers.

'You don't understand how I feel, Jonathan,' she had argued vehemently. 'You've asked me to marry you, but how can I consider it when I don't know who I am?'

'You're just using this as an excuse not to commit yourself to me, Nina,' he had raged. 'What are you afraid of?'

'Please, Jonathan, don't make it worse for me,' she had pleaded. Oh, why had she let their relationship get so far? She was very fond of Jonathan but she wasn't ready for marriage, especially not now. After finding those papers in her adoptive father's bureau, her life was suddenly in turmoil. How could she go ahead with her life when she had this need to know her past before she faced her future?

'You're Nina Parker and you have a mother and a father and they have cared for you all your life,' Jonathan argued on. 'How can you think of doing this to them while they are away?'

Guilt thrummed through her then. Yes, her adoptive parents cared for her, but only in a material way. She couldn't remember a time in her childhood when either of them had ever hugged her or kissed her warmly or even praised her. She was a possession to them, another accessory to their affluent lives.

They had sensibly told her, when she was old enough to understand, that she was adopted, and even at that young age she had begun to understand about feelings—or rather the lack of them. They had made her feel that she should be grateful, rather than fortunate or special, that if they hadn't taken her she would have grown up in an orphanage or a succession of foster homes. From then on the empty, lonely vacuum inside had ballooned, and her parents hadn't had the warmth to fill it for her. She'd been just a pretty little girl to them—

someone to fill the void in their own lives, the daughter they couldn't have themselves—but eventually a disappointment because they couldn't mould her to their way of thinking.

Somehow she had never risen to their expectations, though she had always strived for approval. She had done well at school but it had never been good enough. Both professional people themselves—her mother a teacher, her father a physics lecturer—they had been appalled when she had opted for art school rather than university. She was artistically talented but they wouldn't acknowledge it. They wanted a doctor or a lawyer for a daughter, not an artist who successfully designed and painted quality greetings cards for a living.

And now, while they were away in Australia for a year on an educational exchange scheme, she had found those papers.

'I have a Sicilian father,' Nina reasoned plaintively to Jonathan, 'and my real mother died in a car crash when I was a year old. They told me that but they didn't tell me about my father. I've found those papers and I have a name and a nationality to go on. I want to know my roots, Jonathan. Can't you understand how I feel?'

'You're living in a dream world, Nina—obsessed, even,' Jonathan told her accusingly. 'You could be stirring up a hornet's nest of trouble for yourself and him if you ever find him.'

'That's my problem, my choice!' Nina retorted. 'Anyway, I'm not going to do anything stupid. I just want to find him, just see him, maybe not even speak to him if the conditions aren't right, but I just want to *see* him.'

'You're too soft, Nina, too romantic. I'm damned sure if I had been given away at birth I wouldn't be trying to find my roots now. Your real mother and father obviously didn't want you and—'

'Don't, Jonathan,' Nina bit back, knowing in that mo-

ment of cruelty that Jonathan couldn't really love her
either. To him, too, she was but a possession. If he really
loved her he would support her on this, or at the very
least understand how she felt.

'I just need to know,' she finished weakly. 'Somewhere in Sicily I have a *real* father. I can't really explain
the feeling, but there's a sort of hollow part of me that
needs to be filled. I have a talent, an artistic talent in my
genes, and perhaps I got it from my father. I don't know
and I *want* to know. While Mum and Dad are away in
Australia I'm going to find my real father. I must, don't
you see? Don't you understand? I must *try*!'

But Jonathan hadn't understood, and because of his
lack of feeling and understanding she had ended their
relationship in a final heated exchange of words which
had left him more angry than hurt.

In her heart she knew she had done the right thing in
ending it. But now, miserable and at a very low peak,
Nina was beginning to think he might be right—she was
obsessed with trying to find her father.

Her enquiries had been futile efforts, mainly because
she hadn't done her research properly. She hadn't even
known there wasn't a British consulate in Sicily before
her arrival! She had resorted to telephone directories,
looking for the name Gio Giulianni. She had made a few
calls in the capital, had receivers slammed down on her,
one indecent proposition in broken English—all dead
ends. She had approached some official-looking build-
ings and been laughed at a few times, and the banks had
thrown her out, escorted by security guards. She was
now beginning to realise she had been driven by her
emotions rather than common sense! Just as Jonathan
had said.

And now this, being picked up in the gutter by a complete stranger!

Suddenly they drew into the kerb, the nose of the limo

just nudging into the *piazza*, and with the engine still throbbing as if he couldn't wait to be rid of her. The stranger turned to face her, one hand still resting lazily on the steering wheel, the other coming up to the back of her seat where it stayed. There was a change in his expression. It was almost cynical now, and when he spoke he sounded smoothly cynical. too.

'So, we have arrived at your destination,' he said quietly.

Nina broke the eye contact between them and stared wide eyed at the *piazza* before them, and then she understood his disbelieving cynicism. This wasn't an area where tourists dared venture. Like every big city in every part of the world this one had its down side, too. It was the sort of place travel agents advised you not to venture unaccompanied, if at all. Certainly not a place for little *Engleesh* girls with fascinating long blonde hair, wide, doe-like grey eyes, long, smooth legs shooting out from brief shorts and…and faint hearts.

Nina stared nervously at the collection of swarthy men gathered in the small *piazza*, drinking at the open-fronted bars, waving muscled arms in a typically Mediterranean way. Not a female in sight in this macho square. And there wasn't one man, not one male, she could claim or would *dare* to claim as a boyfriend.

Her heart sank to her scruffy espadrilles. She might have got away with it if she had seen anyone remotely sympathetic. She could have rushed up to a man, preferably a tourist, and hastily suggested that she was in a jam and could he possibly look pleased to see her and just, for the briefest of whiles, *pretend* to be her boyfriend. Just till this enigmatic stranger pulled away and got on with his life, leaving her to get on with her own.

'So,' he breathed, 'which one is it?' He urged her to answer when she made no effort to move. 'Which of these worthy candidates is the boyfriend?' he asked, voice dripping with sarcasm.

'I...I don't think he's here yet,' she uttered weakly.

The thought of getting out of the cocoon of his limo horrified Nina but she had to do it. She'd lost enough face for one day.

'I'll wait,' she said, gathering her backpack from the well in front of her and clutching it to her chest. She reached for the door handle and this time it gave for her. She had one leg out of the car before she remembered her manners. 'Thank you—thank you for helping me.'

She was about to swing her other leg out of the limo when she noticed for the first time Emilio Locasto seated only a few metres away from her. He was sprawled in a white plastic chair under the tatty green awning of a bar, laughing raucously with a group of equally unsavoury friends.

The whole of the events of the morning swam before her eyes. Him coming into her poor excuse for a bedroom that morning as she'd been combing her hair, wondering what horrors would be dished out to her for the day. She'd been hired to look after the children, but washing, scrubbing, cleaning, all the ghastly menial tasks, seemed to have been heaped upon her while the other two maids, distant cousins of the *signora*, played cards in the kitchen while the mistress of the house gossiped in the street.

She had turned from the small mirror she had propped on the high chest of drawers—the only piece of furniture apart from the hard bed—and drawn in her breath with fear as he had firmly closed the door after him. His leering expression had said it all. She had held him off for too long and he wasn't here to be made a fool of any longer.

He had pulled at her thin white cotton vest top, grasped her breast, hurting her so badly she had cried out. Then his mouth was over hers to silence her and he had snatched at her hand and shoved it sickeningly below his waist, so she'd been forced to feel what he thought she ought to crave, and then…then he had toppled her onto the bed and…and then…

Nina fell back into the seat of the limo, clutching at her throat to stem the rise of bile. The world was suddenly spinning, but through the mish-mash of sounds and horrible revived sensations she felt one good thing: a protective arm hauling her further back into the seat, a warm, hard body crossing hers to slam shut the car door and then the comforting sound of the car reversing back along the narrow road that had led to her recalled vision of hell.

She sat trembling beside him and it was an age before she could open her eyes. When she did she was only vaguely aware they were on a wider road, seeming to be heading out of the hot, teeming capital.

'Locasto?' the stranger enquired in a deep, gravelly voice.

She wondered if his query was threaded with anger and he might guess what she had been through and be mad with Locasto, or perhaps mad with her for getting herself into such a situation. But how could he be angry with her? Surely he could see she wasn't that sort of girl, the sort that encouraged married men?

But he didn't know her, and judging by the physical state of her who could guess what sort of a girl she was?

She drew in her bottom lip and stayed silent. To even acknowledge that evil man's existence by offering anything by way of an explanation would reduce her to a gibbering wreck.

'So you don't feel like talking about it,' he uttered, and she wasn't sure if it was a question or a simple deduction.

She stayed silent, too choked up to say anything. She

wanted to forget the Locastos. And at this precise moment she wanted to get as far away from Sicily as was possible. But her predicament was horrendous. If that awful *signora* had paid her it might not be so bad. She would have had some money to build on. Perhaps have got another job and raked up enough for her fare home. Now all seemed hopeless.

Suddenly she couldn't help a small gasp of realisation from bursting from her lips. She turned to him, eyes wide.

'You know him!' she gasped. 'You know Emilio Locasto!'

He only allowed her a small nod of acknowledgement as he steered the limo onto a dual carriageway.

Nina's head spun. A friend of his? Surely not. In the short time she had worked for the Locastos she had sussed that they weren't very nice people to know. The *signore* was some sort of low-life who made a living out of an undoubtedly nefarious trade. They weren't short of money and lived better than most in that particular area; ghastly though the man was, he appeared to have a certain standing in his community.

Her heart quickened. This stranger knew him. Mafia? Were they all up to no good?

She licked her dry lips again. What on earth had she got herself into?

'Um, look, we…we seem to be heading out of the capital, and really…well…if you could drop me back in Palermo… I…I have friends I can meet up with and…' Her voice petered out; she revived with a huge intake of breath. 'I'm very grateful for the lift and you've been most kind—'

'It's all right,' he interrupted smoothly. 'I mean you no harm. I'm no friend of Locasto, though I know him well enough. You need not be afraid of me.'

'I'm not afraid of you,' she blurted. Was she? 'I just…

Where are you taking me?' she ended in a hoarse whisper.

'To my home,' he told her, eyes ahead. 'You need a bath.'

His home! A bath! 'Oh, no,' Nina blurted afresh. 'I am not going anywhere with a stranger who has just hauled me out of the gutter. I might look gullible but I assure you I can handle myself, thank you very much. Now, just you pull up and let me out of here and—'

'And let you get yourself into another mess?'

His voice was scathingly accusing and Nina was riled. She clenched her fists around the silk she was still grasping and opened her mouth to state emphatically that if she chose to get herself into any sort of mess it was none of his business. But before she could get a word across her lips he stilled her with a hand that snaked out to pat her bare knee lightly. She tensed more, his touch like a bolt of electricity on her hot skin.

'Cool it, Nina,' he said lightly, and immediately withdrew his hand. 'You are in no condition to make a decision for yourself at the moment. Just relax and enjoy the scenery and before you know it we will be there.'

He reached forward and switched on the stereo and the limo was filled with the strains of some light operetta, but Nina was in no fit state to appreciate it.

Nina! He had said her name and it echoed and echoed in her ears.

'You…you know my name,' she breathed incredulously.

CHAPTER TWO

HE WAS concentrating on the road ahead now, face as stern as ever, and nervously Nina brought a hand up to relieve the pressure on her throat, where his eyes had eaten her up. Her fingers came into contact with the thin silver necklace and in a sudden heated wave of realisation she snatched at it, breaking the delicate chain.

Idiot, she told herself. That was what Locasto had done to her with his leering looks that had made her flesh creep. A man only had to look at her now and she was fantasising some ghastly encounter of the sexual kind. She was paranoid.

She held the chain in her fingers, smoothing over the pieces of chunkier silver that spelled out her name: NINA. She had bought it in a market on her first day with the Locastos, thinking it would help the children get to know her better. To her dismay, they had used it as a chant. 'Neenah, Neenah,' they had cried hysterically, till all the children in the street had taken it up and taunted her when she ventured out. She had carried on wearing it in defiance.

And the stranger had seen it around her neck. He *didn't* know her. But Locasto didn't wear his name around his neck and the stranger did know *him*, and there was only one way to find out more.

'How do you know him?' she asked.

'Locasto?'

She realised it was quite a while since she had spoken. They were heading out into the country now, the scenery dry. But it was deliciously cool inside the air-conditioned car and it was giving her time to get herself together. For the time being she had nowhere else to go, and seeing the back of Palermo was one good thing out of the day.

'Yes, Locasto,' she murmured.

'I prosecuted him once.'

Nina swallowed hard. 'You're a lawyer?' she asked faintly, her head racing. If he had prosecuted him then he was on the goodies' side surely? And another thought struck her quickly and optimistically. A lawyer knew things other people didn't. He would know the right channels to find her father. The thought made her feel a whole lot better about this curious situation she was in.

'I *was* a lawyer here in Palermo for a while, but I went back to the States a few years ago,' he told her. 'I practise there now.'

'Did you win your case against Locasto?' she persevered, not for a minute imagining this man failing at anything.

He gave her a sidelong thin smile. 'I used to win all my cases.'

'So, what was the situation with Locasto?' he suddenly asked.

Nina went hot all over. He knew him so must have a fair idea what sort of a man he was. And he'd witnessed her eviction, had heard the accusations hurled at her and then her reaction to the sight of that evil man in the *piazza*. It all added up to something distasteful, something she didn't want to go over again.

'There wasn't a situation,' she denied faintly, 'more a misunderstanding.'

From the corner of her eye she saw his brows rise slightly in mock disbelief. Heaven forbid he thought there was no smoke without fire.

'There is no smoke without fire.' He echoed her thoughts and Nina clenched her fists tightly in her lap. Whose side was he on?

'Look, I am very grateful for your help this morning, truly,' she uttered, to change the subject. 'But I think you might be pushing it a bit in taking me to your home.'

Her nerves were beginning to fray again. They were miles out of Palermo now, leaving behind the dusty dry area and heading through more lushly beautiful countryside. Only a few minutes ago she'd been grateful to be seeing the back of the hot capital but now her doubts were worrying her. She really needed to be in town. There was work there. She didn't speak the language but in the tourist areas that wasn't a problem. There was bar work, and she could get another job and start afresh. She had planned on staying another month and perhaps...

'You have no money.' He interrupted her thoughts as if he could read them.

Nina squirmed in her seat. 'I have, and—'

'You wouldn't have been working for the Locastos if you had,' he stated knowingly, with a faint undertone of suspicion which riled Nina once again. Did he really think there was any substance in the *signora*'s accusations? 'I heard you ask for money from the *signora*,' he went on. 'You're a backpacker—alone, too, very dangerous and foolish in any country. You don't look as if you are capable of looking after yourself and I am offering you respite for a while. If I were you, I'd be thanking my lucky stars that I came along in the nick of time.'

Nina flushed hotly at his put down and his arrogance in thinking she should be eternally grateful to him.

'But I don't know you!' she protested angrily. 'You say you are a lawyer but that could be a lie. I don't know do I? For all I know you are no better than Locasto, unable to keep your hands off me,' she ranted on.

His eyes narrowed and his hands stiffened around the steering wheel.

'You've picked me up, caught me when I was at my most vulnerable, and now you are expecting my undying gratitude. Well, I am grateful, but not that grateful,' she ended, hotly and meaningfully.

He shook his head in disbelief, and without looking at her said quietly, 'Take a look at yourself, Nina. I'd have to be hard pressed to accept the sort of gratitude you are suggesting.'

Nina's colour heightened, but no, no, she was not going to be put down a second longer. He might be a devastatingly good-looking, smart-mouthed lawyer, thinking she was mere dirt beneath his chariot wheels, but she had some pride left.

'Not knowing you, how can I be sure? I don't look like this all the time. I don't get pelted with tomatoes in the street every day of my life, and I'm not stupid either. I'm damned sure that if it had been *me* throwing Signora Locasto out into the street you wouldn't have stopped to pick *her* up and offer to take her home for a bath!'

This time he laughed. He had the audacity to laugh at her and Nina's blood raced, and then he said something that nearly floored her. It so completely took her by surprise that her mouth gaped open.

'Oh, Nina,' he chuckled. 'You are all I expected you to be.'

Oh, it was such a weird thing for him to say. A very mysterious remark.

'What do you mean?' she whispered. 'Expected me to be?' she repeated. 'Till just now you had never seen me before in your life. Just who are you anyway?'

He reached into an inside pocket of his jacket, took out a small card and held it out to her. Nina took it and read it avidly, though her heart was suddenly thumping again. Yes, he was a lawyer—Lorenzo Biacci—but the address was a New York one which left Nina none the wiser as to where they might be heading at this moment.

A strikingly good-looking lawyer he might be, but he was still a stranger to her.

With a frown she handed the card back to him and he took it and tossed it lightly onto the dashboard.

'I expected you to be the way you are simply because of your expression when you landed in the gutter,' he told her.

'Oh, yes, and what sort of expression was that?' Nina huffed, still stinging from that embarrassing eviction he had witnessed. No smoke without fire indeed!

His right hand moved from side to side, wavering as if he wasn't quite sure how to describe it. He tried, though. 'Incredulous,' he finally offered, quickly followed by, 'Indignant, too. I saw a fierceness in your pretty little puckered face that said if the odds hadn't been weighted dramatically against you, you might have turned on the *signora* and given her a slap on the face for her trouble.'

'Are you sure you're not a psychiatrist instead of a lawyer?' she quizzed sarcastically.

'Was I right, then?' he asked, serious again.

Nina shrugged. 'I'm not a heroine with odds like that stacked against me. All the women in the street were rooting for her. Besides, Signora Locasto is much stronger than me and even on a one-to-one basis she would probably have flattened me.'

He laughed again and Nina's stomach tightened. His face came alive when he was relaxed. His stone-like beauty became heart-wrenchingly devastating. A man of many facets, she mused, and she saw another when he suddenly became more serious.

'Did she hurt you?' he asked worriedly. He looked at her briefly, eyes narrowed as he took in her dishevelled state, those dark, moody eyes narrowing at the graze on her arm.

Nina covered it with her hand, rubbing away the blood

with her fingers. 'No, I fell against an olive tree and...and, no, she didn't hurt me. I was angry at the injustice of it all more than anything and...and can we leave it alone now? I don't want to talk about it.'

And she didn't. It was bad enough recalling the *signora* bursting into the bedroom, finding her grappling on the bed with her husband and insanely thinking that she was fighting for his attentions rather than fighting *against* them.

'I think you *should* talk about it,' he persisted. 'Besides, I'm curious.'

'Are you indeed?' Nina muttered, and went on muttering under her breath. 'As if I would find that man attractive enough to flirt with him.'

'Ah, I'm beginning to see the picture,' Lorenzo said after a moment's reflection. 'She threw you out because you were making a play for her husband—'

'I was not!' Nina protested. 'She twisted it all around, made out it was me to blame.'

'Maybe you were,' he reasoned. 'You are a very lovely young lady. A temptation to any man.'

'Well, excuse me if I throw that compliment back in your face,' Nina blurted indignantly. 'I didn't ask for anything that happened to me!' She sat tensely, trying to control her temper. How chauvinistic could you get?

Lorenzo suddenly pulled up in a dusty lay-by. Nina could see a village ahead, a pretty red-ochre-roofed village which friendly nationals might inhabit. That would do nicely. It was about time she got her senses together and stood on her own two feet again. He had obviously had more than enough of her this hot morning.

'Thanks for the lift,' she said frostily and went for the door again. Locked again. His arm was up and across the back of hers, and she could feel the heat of his closeness and maddeningly her pulses were racing.

'Now listen to me, Nina. I didn't stop the car to let

you out. I stopped because I have a point to stress. I know you've had a shock and are feeling fragile but don't jump down my throat for the injustice the Locastos have dealt you.'

She lifted her chin. 'And there endeth the first lesson,' she mocked tightly. 'Thanks for the education and thanks for the lift, and would you kindly release this door so I can get out?'

His hand was suddenly on her bare shoulder, warm and firm and...and electrifying. She tensed, but the pressure didn't ease. She tried to gauge the mood of his eyes, because the humour had gone now, but it was useless; she couldn't.

'I'm not putting you down, Nina, not mentally or physically. You are staying in this car. I'm on your side, though in your injured pride you can't see it. But the conversation was enlightening, don't you think?'

'And in what way?' she challenged in surprise.

'Character analysis,' he told her. 'Now you know the sort of man I am. I'm willing to see two sides to every situation and rationalise, whereas you are a very feisty young lady, single-minded, plucky, too, but perhaps a trifle naive. We have now established some sort of rapport and understanding of each other's character and—'

'Just a minute,' Nina interrupted wildly, eyes so wide they hurt. 'Aren't you getting in a bit too deep here? Anyone would think this was an ongoing relationship. We've only just met and suddenly we are delving into each other's pysche—or rather you are delving into mine. Well, once again, thanks for the lift...'

It was useless. She couldn't get out of this car if her life depended on it. His hand suddenly shifted from the backrest of her seat and came up under her hair. A soft, soft caress that truly startled her because of the effect it had on her. It made her blood sizzle alarmingly.

'In a way this *is* an ongoing relationship, Nina. I of-

fered to take you home with me in your hour of need,'
he reasoned softly. 'And I well understand your reluc-
tance to accept my offer graciously so I am trying to
make things easy for us both. It works two ways, you
know. I'm now beginning to wonder if I was in my right
mind in stopping to help you.'

'You have nothing to fear from me!' she blurted
quickly.

'Nor you from me,' he assured her, though he didn't
ease up the soft caress of the back of her neck which
was now doing strange things to her insides. 'Now listen
carefully. Don't keep jumping down my throat; it gets
on my nerves. I fully appreciate your wariness in this
situation but you aren't helping my feelings. You are a
very beautiful young lady, or could be,' he added, his
eyes skimming her poor, dishevelled state. 'And I have
a reputation to preserve, too,' he finalised with huge
pomposity.

With that his hands went back to the steering wheel
and suddenly the car was shooting forward out into the
deserted road ahead.

Dumbstruck, Nina sat as stiff as a rod beside him.
How effectively he had turned that conversation around.
Seeing this situation as a compromising one, *for himself*.
Yes, he was a smart lawyer and, yes, she should be
counting her lucky stars it was him that had stopped to
help, she reluctantly conceded after a few seconds of
sensible reasoning.

'I'm sorry,' she murmured. 'But only sorry for getting
on your nerves,' she quickly added, and not without a
degree of defiant sarcasm. 'The rest of the sermon I can
live without!'

'Accepted,' was his only response.

And nothing more was said for a long while. Though
there was no more conversation, Nina's head was racing.
OK, she was grateful for his courtesy, and if it wasn't

for his wretched arrogance he would be a very interesting, engimatic man. But, attractive or not, he was doing her no favours by whipping her out of Palermo. True, she had nowhere else to go, but she needed the capital. Perhaps after a bath and a short time of respite she might be able to think more clearly. And he was a lawyer, she reminded herself. It would be easy for him to find out the whereabouts of her father so perhaps she had better play it cool for the time being.

Suddenly more at ease with this strange situation, Nina stretched her legs out and tried to relax. Later she would tell him why she was here and perhaps he would help, or at the very least know someone who might.

'Oh, my gosh,' Nina breathed, sitting up and taking interest at last.

The car had slowed to take a small side road that snaked between citrus groves. The lush trees were heavy with fruit, oranges and lemons, and she could imagine the sight and the scents in springtime, when the blossom was at its height. Now the trees laden with fruit were a spectacular sight to a city girl.

A very brown, gnarled, weather-beaten farmer stepped back from the unmade road, dragging a scraggy goat on a length of rope out of the path of the limo. Lorenzo stopped and whirred the electric window down to speak to the man in expressive Italian.

They both laughed and then the car purred forward, the labourer peering in the open window to grin toothlessly at her. Nina hesitantly grinned back with a full set of perfect small white teeth.

'One of my staff,' Lorenzo told her. 'It's an old family estate; hardly profitable, but it gives the local people work.'

The information was given in an unpatronising way and Nina had liked the way he spoke so genially to the old man, and she warmed to him—only slightly, though. She was still a little shell-shocked by his attitude to her and the Locasto fiasco.

The 'old family estate' seemed to run for miles and miles, and it suddenly occurred to Nina that Lorenzo Biacci was a very wealthy man in spite of what he had said about it hardly being profitable.

'You seem to divide your time between here and the States, but why are you back in Sicily now?' she asked as they drove to higher ground, leaving the citrus groves way behind them.

'I had family business to attend to, house staff to liaise with, and a wedding to arrange. I'll return to New York when it's all over,' he told her.

Nina was comforted by the thought that his home would be filled with staff and relatives. A wedding, though. His own?

'Whose wedding? Yours?' she asked brazenly, clenching her fists tightly in her lap.

'No, not mine,' he said with a small smile.

He's already married, Nina thought, mildly disconcerted at the thought and taking a furtive glance at his finger to see if there was a ring. It was bare, but perhaps it wasn't the Sicilian way to wear rings of betrothal. She cleared her throat before asking, 'Do you have a wife already? Children, perhaps?'

His smile was enigmatic. 'No,' was his short reply.

Alarmingly, a frisson of relief rushed through her. She covered the disquieting feeling with a sharp retort. 'No, silly question, really. You would hardly be taking me home for a bath if you were married!'

She blushed after saying that. It almost implied that his intentions weren't quite honourable, and he had already made it quite clear he thought her a mess and not fanciable in the least!

'So now you have a potted history of my life,' he said,

ignoring her crass remark. 'So what about you, Nina? Why exactly are you here in Sicily?'

To Nina's ears the question sounded rather more cynical than a mere query, and she glanced at him to see if his face gave any more credence to what she was thinking. It was impassive as ever but perhaps his lips were a trifle tighter.

Her own lips suddenly tightened defensively. Yes, she needed his help. She had already decided she would ask him for it but...but what? He already thought her foolish and naive. He'd think her all the more naive when she told him she had come to Sicily to find a father she didn't know, armed with only a name and little else.

She was about to admit it all and damn the consequences of what he might think of her when he forestalled her with another question.

'And how come you were working for the Locasto family?'

Oh, it was getting worse. What on earth would he think of her when she told him she had been foolish enough to allow herself to be robbed, had confided her dire circumstances to a girl she had met at the hostel, who had then introduced her to an Italian barman she was seeing, who had told her about the Locastos, who were looking for an English girl to work for them, looking after the children and teaching them English?

Lorenzo Biacci would think even less of her than he thought already, which wasn't very much at all.

And she cared, Nina thought in a troubled moment.

She rubbed her forehead and took a breath. 'I foolishly ran out of money,' she admitted faintly. 'I heard they were looking for someone and...well, I took the job against my better judgement and you know the rest.'

'Which brings us back to the original question,' he sighed. 'What are you here for in the first place?'

'Er, just...well, travelling, really.'

'I don't believe you.'

The remark stunned Nina for a minute. Now he was accusing her of being a liar!

'You said you were meeting a boyfriend in the *piazza*,' he went on, 'and he didn't materialise. Perhaps you had arranged to meet Locasto there and changed your mind at the last minute because you thought I was a better proposition? Just what are you doing in Sicily, Nina?'

Stiff with shock, Nina only just managed to turn her head to gaze at him in alarm. She realised they had come to a halt in front of huge wrought-iron gates. What lay beyond Nina couldn't see, and didn't want to. Her eyes were fixed heatedly on his. Those dark, accusing eyes.

'How dare you? How dare you speak to me like that?' she breathed angrily. 'How dare you think I consider you a better proposition than Locasto? This has gone quite far enough. I refuse to be questioned as if I'm standing in the dock. You take your profession far too seriously. Now let me out of this car immediately.'

He didn't, of course. Their eyes were locked, and suddenly she was acknowledging that this man was powerfully attractive. It was an alien feeling to her. He made her blood rush, her heart flutter, and he was a *stranger*.

Desperately she tried to focus her thoughts on Jonathan, tried to picture his clean cut good looks in her mind's eye, but it was all a blur. Yet she knew if she never saw this man again his features would be branded on her memory for evermore.

'Let me out of this car,' she implored weakly.

He smiled thinly. 'Not, I think,' he murmured, and reached into his breast pocket.

Nina tensed horribly, wondering what he was going to produce. Her eyes flickered with relief when he took out a remote control and aimed it at the electronic gates.

With a whirr of high technology they swung open and Lorenzo drove through.

They were driving very slowly on hot red concrete now, the gates having shut behind them, and what looked like a fortress loomed up, set against the clear blue sky of the horizon. Nina's eyes widened in disbelief. High stone walls stretched east and west and she caught a glimpse of a palatial yellow stone villa ahead, partially screened by majestic pines and poplars.

The whole grandiose effect took her breath away, and for a moment she forgot that a few seconds ago she had demanded to be released.

It was all...all so magnificent: green and lush, the carefully maintained gardens were a feast of colour and exotica. Her eyes hungrily took in the fabulous spectacle of rose gardens, hibiscus and bright geraniums. There were statues spaced along the drive, huge ones, mostly naked men and women, gods and goddesses, and huge antique terracotta urns and pots dripping with exotic flora. It all screamed money and Nina's heart thudded nervously.

She wasn't usually the sort of girl to feel humble, but at this moment in time, bedraggled after her earlier ordeal, still shaken by the effect this man was having on her, she felt as worthy to be here as a bag lady suddenly whipped into the Ritz for a cream tea with a count. So why, why had this man picked her out of the gutter and brought her back to his personal paradise on earth?

They stopped in front of the mellow yellow house and she realised it wasn't a villa at all. It was a very old, elegant, *casa*. Magnificently sprawling, steeped in old-world charm.

She was gaping at the splendid house when Lorenzo turned to her. Suddenly aware he hadn't made a move to get out of the car, she turned her head to look at him again. His features were coldly grim, as were his eyes.

'So, Nina Parker. Here we are and here we stay. I promised you a bath and respite, and I will honour those promises. But I want something more from you.'

Nina's insides tightened with fear and she went hot and cold in quick succession. Her head was spinning. *Nina Parker*. She didn't wear her *surname* around her neck!

He knew who she was.

She was out of the car before she knew it, staring at him with huge questioning eyes. He got out of the car, too, nonchalantly strolling around it to reach in and pick up her backpack.

'You know who I am,' was all she could breathe nervously.

He smiled—without a trace of humour though. 'Yes, I know who you are, but not *what* you are. That will no doubt come out soon enough. Now, shall we go inside and freshen up and get down to business?'

Nina thought she was going to faint. She leaned against the car to steady herself, then leapt back from the burning hot metal as it stung her bare thigh.

He was already striding purposefully towards the oak double doors of his home, and the one comforting thought that kept Nina on her rather unsteady feet was that once he opened those doors an army of servants and a few generations of family would be there waiting.

And she needed to see people because she was beginning to feel like some sort of hostage now. *This man knew her.* He had admitted it. But how could that be?

She was in a compromising position—another one. What sort of *business* had he in mind?

'Just a minute!' she almost screamed as he reached the doors.

He turned and dropped her backpack at his feet. He waited for her to speak and it was some time because

Nina was so confused she could hardly form the words on her dry lips.

'Just…just what is going on here?' she croaked. 'You know me and I don't know you. You…you picked me up in the gutter and…'

And then it hit her. Full in the face, as if she had been punched. Why hadn't she thought of it before? He was someone more powerful than she had imagined. And he had pulled up outside the Locastos not by coincidence but by *intention*.

Lorenzo Biacci had come to get her!

'I…I don't understand,' she whispered feebly.

It was an age till he spoke, an age in which Nina couldn't form a coherent thought in her spinning head.

'Oh, I think you do, Nina Parker,' he said levelly. 'I think you are a lot smarter than the impression you give. Incidentally, what do you do for a living?'

Her lips parted in shock. What on earth had her occupation to do with anything?

'I…I paint—miniatures…animals, flowers, birds… for…for greeting cards,' she found herself uttering.

'Good. There is plenty here to keep you out of harm's way till the wedding is over. Don't worry, once it is you'll be free to leave. And don't worry about money. Once our business is complete and done with you'll have enough to get yourself home, first class, too. I won't sell you cheap.'

With that he turned, lifted her backpack and disappeared into the darkness of his shuttered home, leaving Nina practically frothing at the mouth.

This was ludicrous, she thought in a fury, and obviously a case of mistaken identity. She wasn't the Nina Parker he thought her to be. He had made one huge, scary mistake! He was crazy!

And she was going to tell him so, too. She leapt for-

ward, followed him into the house, and stopped dead in
her tracks in a huge stone-floored reception hall.

No servants. No relatives. Not a soul was waiting in
the cool, darkened hall to meet the master, who stood,
legs apart, arms folded across his chest.

'Welcome to my home,' he said. 'Sadly, no staff. No
one but us.'

'You...you're mad!' Nina breathed faintly, faint
enough for him not to hear. Humour him, she thought
quickly. But how could she joke about something she
knew nothing about? Wedding, what wedding? More to
the point, whose? And what sort of pay-off was he suggesting, and for what? Yes, humour him. But she
couldn't summon a smile to save her life.

Miraculously she was able to move, though. She
stepped towards him on legs that had a will of their own.
She stopped in front of him and lifted her chin to look
him straight in the eye.

'I haven't the faintest idea what all this is about,
Lorenzo Biacci. No doubt I will find out soon enough,
but for the moment how about that bath you promised?
It might have been an excuse to kidnap me, but I need
it. Then you can explain your actions.'

He raised a sardonic black brow. 'No screaming hysterics?' he questioned mockingly.

Then the smile came, and Nina found it quite easy. 'I
leave the hysterics to you, because when you find out
the mistake you have made you are going to feel King
of the Fools.' Her grey eyes flicked over the front of his
silk shirt. 'And, besides, I can't take a man with tomato
pips down the front of his shirt seriously!' she added
flippantly.

Triumphantly she turned away from him and headed
for the wide curving staircase, praying that bathrooms in
Sicilian mansions lived upstairs as they did in most
other houses.

He didn't stop her, and, with as much dignity as a bedraggled nervous wreck could muster, she stepped lightly up the stone steps.

She heard him follow, heard him chuckling to himself, and she bit her lip hard. He was humouring *her*. She wasn't sure who out of the two of them was the craziest. She supposed she would find out soon enough, she thought grimly.

CHAPTER THREE

NINA'S forced bravado sank like a stone as soon as she reached the top of the stairs. The size of Lorenzo Biacci's home took her breath away. Long corridors veered to the east and the west.

She turned to him then, to protest that this was ridiculous and she wasn't who he thought she was, but he was already heading east with her backpack.

Swallowing hard, Nina followed. She was hungry, she realised, quite faint with it. She hadn't eaten since last night, and then only a meagre meal of fish and salad in her basement bedroom. She was so hungry she couldn't think straight. When she had bathed and eaten she would, though, and then she would be out of here as fast as greased lightning.

The corridor was wide and endless with white stone walls and black iron candle sconces to light the way at night but which were unlit now. Terracotta, blue and cream rugs at intervals on the stone walkway broke up and warmed the austerity of stone walls and floors.

Lorenzo stopped at the last oak door and opened it, and light flooded his face. Nina followed him into the room and stifled a gasp of pleasure. If she was to be held hostage here, her suffering would almost be worth it. The bedroom was vast and airy, yet warmly welcoming. Pale yellow walls and rugs on a polished wooden floor gave a feeling of tranquillity. The furniture was antique, ornate but not overly so, and the huge double bed was an inviting cocoon of downy delight, white and frothy with cream drapes suspended from an iron bracket above the bed.

Nina wanted to lie down on it and go to heaven, and forget everything nasty that had happened to her lately.

'The bathroom is over there,' Lorenzo told her with a nod of his dark head. 'I'll leave you to bathe and then come down for breakfast.'

Nina's hand went to her stomach to still it. He must have heard its grumble of neglect.

He smiled. 'I haven't eaten this morning either. I had to make an early start to get into town and—'

'So it wasn't coincidence that you were passing the Locastos at the time of my rapid exit,' she murmured quickly. 'You *had* come to get me.'

'I could hardly anticipate you being thrown at my feet, though,' he told her quietly. 'But, yes, I had come to get you.' He nodded.

'No.' Nina rallied, shaking her head decisively. 'You came to get *a* Nina Parker; and, yes, that is my name. But I'm not the one you think I am. I can't be. You have made some sort of ghastly mistake.'

He shook his head. 'No, Nina, you made the mistake in coming to Sicily to look for your lover. You won't stop this wedding. It goes ahead without you. Now, do as you are told and bathe, and then we will talk and negotiate.'

He left the room smoothly, gliding like some apparition. After the door closed firmly behind him, Nina gave herself a mental and physical shakedown. This wasn't happening. She would wake up in a minute, in some hospital ward, and be told she was suffering concussion after being thrown into the gutter.

According to Lorenzo, she had come to Sicily to stop her lover's wedding. But she *had* no lover. And what sort of negotiations was he talking about? Did he mean to buy her rapid exit from Sicily?

He had made a mistake but he wasn't the sort of man to admit to it. He had told her he was a rational man who saw two sides of things but whether or not he put that philosophy into practice was another thing! She *had* to convince him he had got the wrong person.

She moved to gaze out of the window, across the gardens. It seemed the estate was perched on some hilltop. The sea, blue and sparkling, wavered into the horizon. She didn't know where she was, and she was alone with an enigmatic lawyer who had mistaken her for someone else.

She couldn't believe this had happened. But she was here, that was real. She went to her backpack, pulled her few crumpled clothes from it and tossed them on the bed. She needed a bath and she needed clean clothes.

There was a washing machine in the huge marbled bathroom, a vanity unit, bidet, toilet, a bath and a glass shower cubicle. There was oodles of bathing paraphernalia—oils and lotions and soft springy towels piled on a marble shelf under the window.

The man had style, Nina thought as she stripped off, bundled all her clothes into the machine and set it in motion. Everything was supplied for guests—*willing* guests. She sat on the edge of the bidet and stared morosely at her meagre bundle of clothes swooshing around. But she wasn't a willing guest and this was all so awful, and she wished she had listened to Jonathan and not come to Sicily.

But, if she hadn't she would never have met the strange man whose magnificent house she was in now. She hugged herself tightly and thought about him. The most fascinating man she had ever met. She didn't really want to acknowledge that, but she couldn't help it. Yet somehow it helped because if she had been picked up by an ogre, someone like Locasto, she would have been shivering with fright now. Lorenzo Biacci didn't frighten her, he was just peculiar, but he didn't appear to be the sort of person to make mistakes and he had. She wasn't who he thought her to be.

But there was always a first time for everything, and everyone she supposed as she stepped into the shower. The way she was feeling now a bath might just knock her out for the day, and she needed her wits about her.

An hour later Nina woke up on the downy bed and groaned helplessly. The wicked bed had tempted her and she had only lain on it for a minute after her shower to get her head sorted.

Three seconds into consciousness she sat bolt upright, snatched at the lacy bedcover and whipped it up around her nakedness. A jug of freshly squeezed orange juice and a crystal glass were on the bedside table and they hadn't been there before!

She stifled a gasp as the door suddenly opened and Lorenzo stepped into the sun-drenched room. What use the cover clutched tightly to her chest now? He had already been in the room while she slept naked. Her skin fizzed at the thought that he couldn't have failed to look at her while she slept!

As if she wasn't there, he strode across the room and pulled the drapes across the window, dulling the room.

'To keep the sun and the heat out,' he told her.

Nina stared at him, so embarrassed she couldn't speak. He had shed his jacket and changed his shirt and looked fresh and crisp—whereas she, in spite of the shower and shampoo, still felt dishevelled. She had been so weary she hadn't combed her hair after washing it, allowing it to dry naturally on the pillow, so it was now fluffy and out of control.

'I hope you feel better now,' he said as he came across the room to her.

'Yes, thank you,' she managed to murmur. Then, raking her hair back from her face with one hand, she sighed deeply, feeling like Goldilocks caught by Papa Bear. 'Look, I'm sorry for taking advantage and sleeping, but—'

He lifted a hand to still her apologies. 'I understand and it's OK but I think you might have a dressing problem. I couldn't help noticing that all your clothes are in the washing machine. But perhaps that was the idea,' he added mysteriously.

Nina couldn't see what he was getting at. Her eyes widened innocently. His took on a frown.

He stood over the bed looking down on her, big and dark and slightly menacing. 'Don't take me for a fool, Nina,' he warned darkly. 'This sort of behaviour might turn your lovers on but I'm made of sterner stuff. A naked woman sprawled on the bed with dappled sunlight accentuating every delicious curve certainly made my blood rush, but then I reminded myself of how dangerous you are. It soon cooled my ardour.' He smiled then, a curious twisted smile that had Nina's heart racing with indignation and embarrassment.

He thought she had fallen asleep naked on purpose, to tempt him! She controlled her anger and smiled sweetly. 'You sure have me down as some sort of vamp, don't you? Well, let me enlighten you, Lorenzo Biacci. I wouldn't come on to you if you were the last man on earth. I thought you were quite a gentleman at first but familiarity certainly breeds contempt!'

Nina pushed back the cover of the bed and, naked, nerves quaking inside, she swung her legs over the edge and got to her feet. 'So, now you've seen it all, and in spite of what you say I'm sure that me seeing *you* naked at some time could be easily arranged! Now excuse me.'

She swept across the room and with dignity opened the door of the bathroom and slammed it after her. Then she collapsed back against it, biting her knuckles hard, her whole body convulsing into shivers of embarrassment and shock at her own behaviour. Where was her nerve coming from? This wasn't like her at all! But he made her that way. Made her so angry she lost control!

She grabbed at a towel and hugged it around her. Oh, God, what had she done and said? Cavorting around naked and saying such things.

She heard the door of her bedroom slam shut. Helped by hand or a gust of wind, she wasn't sure. She breathed evenly at last and cursed herself for being such a fool as to have tossed *all* of her clothes into the washing machine. She hadn't a thing to wear!

She opened the now still machine and hauled her clothes onto the tiled floor to sort them. A thin cotton top and shorts would take at least an hour or two to dry, and—

She heard the click of the bedroom door again and froze against the back of the bathroom door.

'There's a dress on the bed,' she heard Lorenzo call out. 'Come down when you are ready.'

Nina waited a full five minutes after the door closed after him before venturing out and peering fearfully around the bedroom in case he hadn't left after all. She clasped a towel around her and her eyes settled on a gorgeous pale blue silk dress with a watery pattern of paler blue drifting across the expensive fabric draped over the end of the bed. Tentatively, Nina lifted the slip of a dress and held it against her. It would fit perfectly.

In confusion she lifted the label. It was designer and expensive and came from New York, and her heart tightened angrily. He might not be married but he had a lady back in New York. A lady who was intimate enough with him to leave clothes here in his Sicilian home. She flung the dress contemptuously across the bed. He had some nerve, expecting her to wear it.

An hour later Nina ventured downstairs. She wore her own clothes. She had hung her thin white cotton shirt out of the window to dry in the hot sun, likewise a floaty cinnamon-coloured skirt. The waistband was still damp but she didn't care; anything was better than wearing his lady's clothes. The rest of her damp clothes she had bundled into a polythene bag and into her backpack along with the rest of her belongings, only pausing briefly and regretfully over her watercolours and brushes. She would have been in her element painting everything in sight at his beautiful home but that wasn't to be after she had had her say.

She found him at the back of the house, sitting at a white wrought-iron table on a terracotta-tiled terrace that overlooked the gardens. He had some paperwork laid out in front of him and was working under the shade of a vine canopy, bunches of purple grapes dripping from it. He had a glass of wine at his elbow and she vaguely wondered if it was made from the previous year's grapes.

'I'm ready to leave now,' she told him firmly. She had drunk the juice he had left for her and felt much stronger than before. 'I'm afraid I must impose on you further by asking you to drop me at the nearest main road. I'm sure under the circumstances of your grave mistake you won't refuse,' she told him confidently.

She stood stiffly by the table, waiting for him to lift his arrogant head and acknowledge her presence. He did at last. He looked her up and down, scathingly, and smiled ruefully.

'You are a surprise. I thought you would have leapt at the chance of wearing an expensive dress. You might at least have ironed those before putting them on. Have you no pride?' His voice dripped mockery.

Nina lifted her chin. 'It's because I do have pride I chose to wear my own crumpled, still slightly damp clothes, rather than your lover's cast-offs,' she told him stiffly.

His eyes narrowed and wearily he let the gold fountain pen he was holding drop from his fingers. 'You really haven't got the point of all this, have you, Nina? You are not going anywhere—yet,' he added with emphasis. 'We have some bargaining to do before the wedding, and after you can leave. I'm not risking you out of my sight till it is all over.'

'Ah, yes, this mysterious wedding,' Nina said sharply. 'Look, I don't know who or what you are talking about, and to be perfectly honest I'm not interested. I just want to get out of your space and get on with my life.'

'Get on with your enquiries, you mean.' He sighed and got up from the table, shuffling papers as he went on. 'I'll save you the trouble of trying to find him. He doesn't want to be found, Nina. Your brief affair is over. He is going to marry the woman he loves and there is nothing you can do about it. I know rejection can be a painful experience, but you are young enough to put it behind you and find someone more fitting to your way of life. Thrusting yourself at him at this moment, only weeks before the wedding, will do no one any good and—'

'Stop it!' Nina cried. She couldn't bear any more. This was all nonsense. She didn't even know who he was talking about. Someone who was getting married, obviously, but who? No one she knew, because she knew no one in Sicily. 'I don't know who you are talking about. I haven't been rejected and—'

'Yes, well, they all think that,' Lorenzo interrupted, shaking his head in disbelief.

'And who are *they*? Women, I suppose?' Nina said scathingly, going off on a tangent in this peculiar conversation. 'You, Mr Lawyer, know nothing about women, absolutely zilch!' she finished hotly.

Her outburst left her feeling extremely weak, but not so weak that she wasn't able to dredge up something from his wild dialogue. Continue her enquiries? She *had* been making enquiries before he had come into her life to upset it so. She'd been trying to trace her father. But of course he didn't know that. And how could she ask for his help now? He was totally unapproachable. He thought she was someone else, someone not very nice by the sound of it.

She reached down for her backpack, which she had dropped at her feet. 'I'm leaving now,' she went on fiercely. 'You can't stop me. You're a lawyer so must know you can't hold someone against their will. Forget the lift. I'll go under my own steam, but go I will.'

He caught her before she had a chance to turn away. He grasped her upper arms so determinedly the bag dropped from her hand. Her eyes met his and her nerve nearly failed her.

'My God, you are some determined lady,' he seethed through his gritted teeth. 'What is it going to take to make you see reason? Money—how much?' he challenged darkly.

Nina parted her lips with shock. Reason, money? He *was* crazy. His eyes suddenly fixed on those parted lips and devoured them with such depth that Nina braced her whole body in his grip. Oh, no, he looked as if he was going to kiss her and…and that was ridiculous. Her eyelashes flickered nervously; her insides twisted at the thought of those lips coming down to hers and sending her to heaven.

And suddenly a small smile teetered on the edge of his mouth, a small smile of realisation.

'Ah, yes,' he murmured. 'You've named your price.'

His mouth was suddenly on hers, not taking Nina at all by surprise, but the depth of the kiss did. It shocked her rigid. It was hot and deep and so engulfing she thought she might drown in the wave of thrilling sensation it swirled down her spine. He held her so commandingly there was no escape, his arms were around her body like a vice. And as her bones melted and her head reeled dizzily she was astonished to realise she didn't want to escape. She wanted to drown in sensuality, float to the moon in ecstasy. She never wanted it to end.

If she had ever needed proof of sexual chemistry this was it, her senses reasoned tremulously. He thought her a vamp, she thought him out of his mind. She angered him, he angered her. They didn't know each other, they didn't even *like* each other, but that odd feeling she had had in the car with him had pointed the way to this. A kiss to end all kisses.

She was senseless in his arms, soft and vulnerable. His mouth moving across hers so erotically was scary but…but she didn't fight it. She didn't give in to it either. He was arrogant enough without him thinking this was having any effect on her.

Dizzily she was suddenly aware of a sound behind her. His mouth was still devouring hers but she felt it tighten, thin and then very slowly draw away from her. The noise, a low, low growl, was definitely behind her so it wasn't coming from Lorenzo Biacci!

'Stay perfectly still,' he warned against the flush of her cheek, without releasing her from his grasp.

He said something rapid and halting in Italian over her shoulder and then repeated it more fiercely when the growl deepened.

It was a dog, a huge one by the sound of the depth of the warning growl, Nina realised, and she tried to twist out of Lorenzo's grasp to look, but his grip on her tightened and his body was stiff against hers.

He's terrified of it, Nina thought quickly, surprised and amused too. But dogs held no fear for Nina. She had always adored them, and had pleaded for one as a child but without success. Her mother loathed animals.

She twisted again and was successful this time, free of Lorenzo clinging to her.

The dog *was* huge, the biggest and fiercest-looking German shepherd dog she had ever seen in her life. It stood shaggily solid, all black and tan, at the top of the terrace steps, and its teeth were bared dangerously, its warning growl like rolling thunder.

Nina squatted down next to Lorenzo, held her hand out to the dog and called the animal to her.

'Here, boy,' she called softly.

The growling stopped instantly but then Lorenzo reached out a protective hand to grip her shoulder, as if to pull her out of the way. As soon as his hand made contact with her the growling started again.

'Let me go,' Nina warned him in a low, urgent whisper. 'He's warning you off, not me. I know you are afraid of him but I'm not and he knows.'

Reluctantly Lorenzo released her, indignantly muttering under his breath that he wasn't afraid, only afraid for her.

'Oh, yeah,' Nina muttered, unconvinced.

The huge dog, suddenly a big, hairy softy, loped towards her.

Nina reached out her hands, grasped him by his ears and rubbed them lovingly.

'Oh, you are a beautiful boy,' she cooed enthusiastically. 'Where did you come from?'

'He only understands Italian,' Lorenzo told her stiffly.

As soon as he spoke the dog bared its teeth again and growled, its glassy brown eyes menacingly directed at the lawyer as he stood rigidly over the two of them.

Nina lifted her hand and sharply tapped the dog on the nose to quieten him.

'Now, you stop that this minute,' she warned him firmly. 'It's just not friendly to your master. You be a good boy and roll over and let me tickle your tum.' She helped him by pushing at his side, and heard a sharp intake of disbelieving breath from Lorenzo as the dog flopped onto the hot terrace tiles and rolled onto his back.

Nina laughed with delight and rubbed furiously at the dog's tummy till his legs kicked with ecstasy. She turned her face up to see Lorenzo's reaction. He was holding his forehead as if suddenly stricken with a migraine.

'I have a way with animals,' she told him with a grin.

'I've noticed,' he said ruefully, drawing fingers frustratedly through his hair. 'That creature is *supposed* to be a guard dog.'

'He is,' Nina told him with a laugh. 'Mine, obviously. Let that be a warning to you.'

She stood up and faced him then, the smile gone from her lips now, a puckered frown on her hot brow. The arrival of that big hairy thing at her feet, supposedly a ferocious guard dog, had defused what had just happened—Lorenzo having the audacity to take her in his arms and kiss her that way. Now that feeling flooded back to her as a warning. She was in enough trouble without him thinking she was a push-over in the emotional stakes.

The kiss had been an outrageous assault on her senses but best she didn't make too much of it. However, he needed to be told. This morning he had arrived in Palermo and rescued her like a guardian angel, so she had thought. It seemed she had a new one now, a soft-as-butter German shepherd dog who had come to rescue her when a certain lawyer was taking advantage of a moment of idiocy, a kiss.

'If you try that again with me you know what you are in for from him,' she warned Lorenzo, nodding in the direction of the ecstatic dog, who was still rolling helplessly on the tiles.

A thin smile spread across his mouth at her warning.

'He's usually penned, but he must have heard your voice, thought you a soft touch and chewed his way out. I doubt he could chew through a locked oak door, though,' he said, one daring black brow raised knowingly.

Nina came over very hot indeed. She clenched her fists tightly. 'If by that veiled threat you mean a bedroom door, think again because I'm not going to be here,' she told him frostily. 'I've had quite enough of this nonsense and I'm leaving.'

Determinedly she bent and picked up her backpack, which set the dog off whining miserably. Nina stared at it in disbelief. The silly animal didn't want her to go. Already they were friends for life.

'Sorry, darling. I have to go,' she murmured. 'Remember what I said and be a good boy for your master and—'

'He's not mine,' Lorenzo interrupted, plunging his hands into the pockets of his trousers and seeming to rock on his heels. 'Hence the animosity between us,' he added nonchalantly. 'He belongs to the housekeeper, who is away working at the other house in preparation for the wedding.'

'Oh,' Nina breathed with a frown. 'Well, I hope you are giving him tender loving care while she is away. Instead of keeping him penned, which is very frustrating for a dog of his size, why not let him roam free? Then you'd have a chance of winning him over,' she advised tartly.

'I have better things to do with my time than wet nurse a dog.'

Nina didn't like his attitude at all. 'You *are* looking after him properly?' she asked with concern.

Lorenzo carelessly shrugged his wide shoulders. 'I toss him some scraps from time to time.'

Appalled, Nina gasped. 'And exercise? You have to allow a dog of that size plenty of exercise!'

Lorenzo shrugged again.

Nina's eyes widened with distress. She couldn't bear the thought of this lovely animal being neglected. 'You're wicked,' she blurted emotionally. 'How could you be so cold towards him? He is wary of you because you distrust him. Dogs know these things. If I was staying I would make sure he was fed and watered and exercised properly, and I'd make sure he was loved and—'

'But you are determined to leave, aren't you?' he interjected smoothly, leaning towards her to emphasise his point. 'So if you go you will never know his fate, will you?' he added drily.

Nina's backpack thudded to the ground again as she gazed at him in alarm. He wasn't serious, surely?

Lorenzo was watching her face, a slight brightness to his eyes that had Nina's doubts about him wavering, and suddenly the light dawned and Nina got the message.

'You are just trying to frighten me, aren't you?' she blurted knowingly. 'You're making out you don't care about him so I will stay.'

This time he simply shrugged without saying a word. Nina hesitated. So how could she be sure if he was serious or not? She couldn't. She didn't know him well enough. She could call his bluff and walk away, but... The dog was suddenly sitting on her feet, gazing up at her imploringly, his left paw held up in front of him, pleading with her.

Nina gazed down at the dog with wide eyes. Leave the big softy to his fate? If his fate was what Lorenzo was hinting at, neglect! But surely not. The man was intelligent, caring in a way. Whatever lay behind this mistaken identity business it could all be worse. He could have locked her in a darkened cellar and fed her bread and water till this wedding was over—the wedding of a man she was supposed to have had a brief affair with. But the accommodation was sublime, and the food…well, he wasn't going to starve her, but she hadn't seen any food yet so…

'Oh, this is all ridiculous,' she retorted to Lorenzo, still unsure of how he really felt about the dog, but sure that she wasn't going to fall for some sort of emotional blackmail and stay.

'I think Carlo agrees.'

Nina gazed back at the dog. His head was to one side now, just like some cartoon dog, trawling for sympathy. His left paw landed softly on her thigh and he let out what sounded remarkably like a pleading sigh.

Nina refused to give any weakness away to the dog, though her heart had melted on sight of him and the clever dog probably knew that anyway. She folded her arms across her chest and tilted her head to look Lorenzo in the eye.

'You know, a while ago you were determined I wouldn't leave here, but now you are using this dog as emotional blackmail to try and keep me here against my will. That surprises me. Losing your bottle, are you?' she taunted. 'Losing faith in your own ability to keep me here against my will?'

'I have every faith in myself,' he told her levelly, a teasing smile gathering at the corner of his mouth. 'In a court of law I use every emotional tactic I can get my hands on to win my cases. In this particular case I don't need it because what I say goes. But perhaps a bit more emotional weight might make *you* feel happier about the situation. While you are here you can look after Carlo for me. It will give you something else to occupy yourself with.'

Nina stared at him in disbelief. 'Honestly!' she huffed in indignation. 'You really have got a nerve!'

At their heated exchange, Carlo gave out a high-pitched yowl.

Lorenzo's smile broadened. 'Now see what you have done—upset the dog. If you want to avoid stressing him further I'd advise you to stop fighting me and do as I tell you. Now, while you and he bond some more I'll go and fix us some lunch, and unless you want him slobbering all over you while we eat I'll give you some more advice. Take him back to his pen.' He waved his hand across the terrace wall in the direction of the gardens and then strode into the house after gathering up his papers in one purposeful swoop.

Nina watched his retreat with wide eyes. She was sorry her vocation in life leaned towards the artistic rather than the academic because she felt she had well and truly lost that case. She'd never have made law school! In horror she stared down at Carlo. 'This is all your fault,' she reprimanded him hotly. 'And who's going to stop *him* slobbering over me when you're not around,' she added worriedly. She wouldn't be able to bear it if Lorenzo did that again, kissed her so sensuously. But she wasn't staying anyway so it wouldn't happen!

Carlo wagged his tail energetically and whined at her.

'You do understand English, don't you?' Nina said on a worried sigh. 'Pity Lorenzo Biacci doesn't,' she went on ruefully. 'He just won't take no for an answer.

She sighed again and pulled herself together. Somehow she would convince Lorenzo he was wrong and then he would allow her to leave. It was best she did, and the sooner the better now that things were going from bad to worse.

'Come on, Carlo.' She grinned down at him. 'Show me where you live and then let me get back to my lunch. I'm starving if the truth be known. I can think better on a full stomach and once I've talked him round I *will* be leaving.' She ruffled the thick fur on his head. 'Pity I can't take you with me but you must stay here with him. He's mad, of course, but then you already know that, don't you? I didn't come here to cause trouble. He thinks I'm someone terrible and I've come to stop a wedding. Well, I expect you know more about that than I do. Pity you can't speak; you might be the only one around here that talks any sense!'

Carlo listened intently, one ear cocked, and then his appealing brown eyes looked past her and Nina turned to follow the dog's gaze.

Lorenzo Biacci was leaning in the open door, arms across his chest. He looked as if he had been there long enough to hear every word she had said to Carlo. His face was as expressionless as ever, though. She supposed he was trained not to give anything away. He had given something away earlier, though. He had kissed her, given a great deal of ardour to it too. He might have thought that was her price and been acting on it, whatever that might mean, but he had been as lost in it as she had and that was a chink in his armour, though how she could use that to her advantage she hadn't the faintest idea.

She turned her troubled gaze away from him and with a sharp whistle between her teeth she stepped lightly over to the terrace steps. Carlo was already ahead of her, his claws clinking on the steps as he bounded happily down them.

Nina turned once before descending into the gardens. Lorenzo was still there in the doorway, watching her, assessing her. Thinking maybe he had made a mistake after all? Who could tell what he was thinking? But whatever it was Nina hoped it wasn't all bad. When all this mess was over with and he realised his mistake perhaps she would still be able to ask for his help, because in spite of this confusion with him she was still determined to find her father.

She followed Carlo, not so hurriedly now, more pensively in fact. The need to know still burned inside, more so now, she realised as she gazed around the sweeping gardens in awe. This was such a beautiful country—her heritage. Her father was here somewhere and she *had* to find him.

'I'm convinced now,' Nina told Lorenzo when she got back to the shady terrace half an hour later. He was sitting waiting for her, a buffet meal laid out on the wrought-iron table under the vine canopy. Nina slumped into the chair across from him and started to help herself to salad and cold meats. 'That was all bluff on your part,' she went on. 'Carlo has a wonderful kennel, plenty of shade under his own olive tree, plenty of water and a run you could gallop a small pony in. Even if he is your housekeeper's dog this is still your home and you have provided well for him.'

She started to eat. The tomato, olive oil and basil salad was delicious, freshly prepared, too. She lifted her head to see why he wasn't saying anything. He was leaning back in his seat, just watching her with those dark, hooded eyes of his. He hadn't started to eat but was nursing a glass of wine in both hands, just watching her.

In embarrassment Nina let her fork down onto her plate. 'I'm sorry,' she muttered. 'I should have waited. Do...do you want to say grace or something?'

Lorenzo's eyes widened in surprise and then he smiled thinly.

'You are ever a source of amazement to me,' he said quietly. 'I can see the attraction, though—bubbly young blonde, effervescent as young wine. He must have been bowled over by you. But a grave mismatch. The age difference is the real problem, though.'

Nina sat as still as a cornered mouse. Was he talking about her supposed lover? She wanted to protest, yet again, that he had the wrong bubbly blonde, but her curiosity was aroused and she waited, sensing more.

'I can understand your attraction to him, too,' he went on. 'An older, mature, strikingly powerful man. But Gio Giulianni has one weakness: women. You are no good for him but Sofia is. They should have been married years ago, but...'

Nina's eyes widened painfully. Her heart tightened and her spine froze. *Gio Giulianni*. He was talking about her father! The blood seemed to drain from her veins. She felt sick and faint and clenched her damp palms together on her lap.

'I know this must be painful for you,' she heard through a long echoey tunnel, 'but it is best you know.'

But she didn't want to know. She didn't want to *know*! Oh, God, why had she come? Why hadn't she listened to Jonathan?

'Here, drink some water. You look a little pale.'

Eyes wide with shock, Nina watched him through a haze as he poured her a glass of iced water from a carafe. She took the glass, her fingers trembling.

'I'm sorry,' she heard him murmur, and he genuinely sounded as if he was—though for what, Nina wasn't sure.

Nina drank thirstily. In a daze, she put the glass down on the table. If her head suddenly spun from her shoulders she wouldn't be at all surprised. Her father was going to be married and Lorenzo Biacci thought she was his mistress. What sort of a person did that make her father? What sort of a person did Lorenzo think her to be, pursuing a man old enough to be...to be her father?

The very thought churned her stomach and made her feel so very wretched, and she didn't want to be here...wished with all her might that she had never found those papers and blindly and thoughtlessly...yes, thoughtlessly...wanted to find him.

She had come to Sicily to find a father she didn't know but Lorenzo had found her first. He believed her to be a woman scorned—scorned by her own father. And her father would scorn her if he ever found out she was here. The last thing he wanted around at this moment in time was an illegitimate daughter he had probably forgotten about!

'I...I have to go,' she managed to say haltingly. She tried to stand up but couldn't manage it. Her legs were like lead, her insides like jelly.

'You know that isn't possible,' she heard him say. 'I can't take the risk of you finding him and causing a scandal. You are not wanted, not needed. It's my duty to keep you out of the way so you can do no damage.'

Her heart tightened cruelly. She wanted to protest but couldn't because it hurt so much to hear those words. She wasn't wanted.

Bravely she lifted her face to look at the man who had just delivered her the biggest blow of her life. He was gazing at her in a warning way, eyes narrowed and very, very dark, actually believing she was capable of such a thing—the vengeful mistress syndrome. That hurt, too, terribly so, and Nina wished with all her heart it didn't, because, all said and done, why should she care what he thought of her? But she did, damn it, she did.

CHAPTER FOUR

'How did you find me?' Nina asked at last, her voice such a scratchy whisper it was barely audible. She was in such a shocked state she didn't know what else he had said about her father, if anything. The heat was suffocating her, the shock to her system at what she had just heard so debilitating she wondered if she would ever feel right again.

'My housekeeper and Gio's housekeeper are sisters,' he explained. 'You called Gio's home and she answered. The rest you can guess.'

She was shocked to hear she had come that close to finding her father. One of those telephone calls she had made had hit home. What if her father had answered the phone? What would she have said? Whatever, she wouldn't be here now, hearing all Lorenzo's painful accusations and suffering this way.

'I...I didn't say my name,' Nina faltered, knowing she hadn't. What exactly she had said on those numerous phone calls she'd made she couldn't remember, because she had been so nervous, but she'd never given her name.

'Under the circumstances you wouldn't, would you?'

Nina looked at him sharply, despising him for his suppositions.

'So, I repeat, how did you know who I was and how did you find me?' she asked him coldly.

'Because your enquiries took you to places I have connections with. I'm known in Palermo and have friends. Palermo is a big city yet a small one. I started to make my own enquiries. It wasn't long before I had your name and the address where you were working.'

Nina lifted her hand to smooth the dampness from her brow. Yes, she supposed for him that was easily done.

'And...and Gio, he...he instructed you to get rid of me?' she asked in a small, thin voice. It was an appalling thought. *Get rid of the mistress before my wedding.* What sort of a man was her father?

Nina lifted her head because Lorenzo hadn't answered her. He was leaning over the table, helping himself to the food, adding more to her own plate.

'You must eat,' he told her softly.

'Eat—how can I eat?' she blurted. Her hands stayed clenched tightly in her lap. If she clenched them tightly enough and wished very hard perhaps she could spirit herself away from here. She tried to relax, because without the tension she might be able to think rationally and not feel so pained at this experience.

Oh, she had wanted to know her father so badly. She hadn't wanted to cause anyone any harm, and wouldn't have done. She had only wanted to fill that vacuum inside her. But did her feelings matter any more after finding out what she had?

'You...you haven't answered me,' Nina went on. 'Did...did he instruct you to get rid of me?'

'Does it matter?'

His tone was so offhand it infuriated Nina. She wanted to hit out at him for his crassness, but of course he didn't know the truth. He just supposed she was the lover come to stop the wedding. She fought very hard to calm herself down and try to understand his position, but it wasn't easy.

'Why are you doing this?' she asked quietly. 'What interest do you have yourself in all this? You won't admit that my...that Gio instructed you to pay me off, so I presume you must be doing this for yourself.' But why should he do that?

He leaned across the table again and poured a glass of sun-drenched Chardonnay for her. Nina ignored it. She needed a clear head, not a muzzy one.

'I told you before, Gio is going to marry the woman he should have married years ago. My interest in all this is that I want the wedding to go smoothly.' He leaned back then, and looked at her directly.

Nina met his gaze and held it, sensing he was going to tell her more—and she wanted to know it all, every last, ghastly detail.

'Gio is my closest friend,' he went on levelly, his eyes dark and meaningful. 'I love him like a father because I haven't one of my own. I know him well enough to know that he doesn't need you around at this sensitive time of his life.'

'So...so he didn't start all this? This is all coming from you,' Nina accused, angry that he should be interfering in such a way, angry that he should love *her* father when he had no such right. 'Don't you think you are taking on a bit much, especially as you know so little about it all?'

He knew absolutely nothing, as it happened, Nina thought miserably, and she was hardly in a position to enlighten him. She wasn't Gio's lover; she was his illegitimate daughter. Spring that on the lawyer and he might have her thrown out of the country sooner rather than later.

'I know enough to want to avoid any trouble,' Lorenzo said quietly.

His dark look was meaningful, questioning her. Even if she denied being the mistress he thought her to be it would open a new can of worms. He would want to know just why she had been trying to find the man if it wasn't for reasons of stopping the wedding, or at the least causing a disturbance. Mistress or daughter? Nina tried to reason what could be worse—either/or? A mistress certainly wasn't wanted around at the groom's wedding; that was understandable. But a daughter, an illegitimate daughter... Was that worse?

'I didn't come to Sicily to cause any trouble,' Nina murmured softly, lowering her head to gaze bleakly at her white knuckles clenched in her lap. And it was true, she hadn't. She had vowed to walk away at any sign of trouble if she located her father and the circumstances weren't right for a meeting. And she wanted to walk away now, but that was looking impossible with Lorenzo Biacci's determination to keep her here in his home, out of harm's way.

She shrugged helplessly and muttered hopelessly. 'I...I just wanted to see him.' But how hopeless now. Lorenzo Biacci wouldn't allow her within a thousand miles of him. She was trapped here, would be guarded till the wedding was over and then she would be sent post-haste back to where she had come from.

Nina squeezed her hands tighter. To come so close, so very close, to finding him, only to have it all snatched cruelly from her and in such a painful way. To be accused so...

But...but if her father met her he would know that she wasn't his mistress. He would know he had never set eyes on her before, he would know that Lorenzo had made a mistake. Nina quaked inwardly. Then the explanations would have to unfold, and...

Bravely Nina lifted her head and looked at Lorenzo, who was watching her silently, motionlessly, giving nothing of himself away.

'T-tell me,' she whispered. 'Were there others? You...you said he...Gio...you said his weakness was women. I mean...'

'What *do* you mean?' Lorenzo breached her faltering

questions. His tone was abrasive, his dark eyes suddenly hostile, as if she shouldn't ask such confidences. 'Surely you are not naive enough to think your relationship was serious?'

Nina drew in her lower lip and looked away from him. It was horrible, him thinking this way about her. Taking it for granted that because she had been making enquiries about Gio Giulianni she was a mistress.

Where her strength came from she didn't know, but somehow it was there for her when she needed it. She settled her eyes on him again, cool grey eyes that had learnt a lot from him. She wasn't giving anything away either.

'Mistresses come second in the naivety stakes, second to wives. If there were other women in Gio's life I never knew,' she told him truthfully.

But she did need to know more about her father. Just something to help her on her way. Perhaps it would help to know that her father was a philanderer, a breaker of women's hearts. Perhaps it would help to know he wasn't a nice man to know. Then she could go home and count her blessings and be glad, yes, glad that her real parents had given her away.

'Gio has a dark past,' she heard Lorenzo offer. 'I doubt anyone other than myself has his full confidence. You might have shared his bed at some time but you would never know his deepest thoughts, no woman ever has.'

Nina closed her eyes in suffering. Could it get more painful? And yet she couldn't help wanting to know more.

'This dark past of his...' she started, but a snort of derision from Lorenzo put a stop to what she wanted to ask.

'No way, Nina, you're not going to get anything more

out of me. Let's leave Gio alone now, shall we, and—?'

'No,' Nina protested quickly. 'That's not fair. You brought me here to keep me out of his way. You've made all these accusations and now you want to drop the subject. You can't turn my world upside down and then just close off. I mean, it's not fair and...'

She rubbed her forehead fiercely. She was getting far too emotional now and asking the impossible of him but, oh, how much she wanted to know.

'You really care for him, don't you?' Lorenzo said quietly. 'Perhaps you really are in love with him.'

Nina forced herself to look at him, her eyes wide and on the very brink of tears. She would have liked the *chance* to love him. Not in the way Lorenzo supposed, though.

'Perhaps I am,' she murmured evasively as stiffly she got to her feet.

'Where are you going?'

Nina took a deep breath of warm, fragrant air and lifted her face to gaze across the terrace wall and beyond.

'Just for a walk,' she told him, and tried to force a smile, to act as normal as possible. He'd hit her with a sackful of emotions she was finding difficult to cope with and she needed air and solitude to think about them.

'I'll come with you.'

He went to get up but Nina stilled him by lifting her hand.

'Please don't.'

He was watching her again, that curious, penetrating look, as if he was trying to get into her very soul.

'I'm not going to try and get away,' she went on sombrely. 'I accept everything you have said, and I repeat, I didn't come to Sicily to cause any trouble and I won't. I need time to think, that's all.'

'Nina.' His voice was thick and for once he didn't meet her eyes directly. He was seated at the table, toying with a silver fork and staring down at it as he twirled it between finger and thumb. 'You didn't know about the wedding till I told you, did you?'

And now he was sounding as if he felt sorry for her, as if he had been the bearer of bad news about the man she loved.

'No, I didn't,' she admitted softly. She hadn't even known who he was talking about at first. She smiled ruefully. Not in her wildest dreams could she have foreseen this. Coming to Sicily in time for her father's wedding day. A wedding she wouldn't and couldn't be a part of.

'I won't lose any sleep over it, though,' she told him bravely, and he lifted his head and looked at her in surprise.

And to cover the hurt and the shock and the awfulness of it all she became daring and flippant. 'Sofia, this woman he should have married years ago, is welcome to him. Somehow I don't envy her. It sounds as if she might have her hands full keeping him in control.' She flicked an errant strand of fair hair from her brow and smiled at the lawyer. 'As for me, I'm a survivor. No broken heart, no hurt feelings. Plenty more fish in the sea, as they say.'

She went to turn away, masking those hurt feelings she had just denied she felt, but a long drawn out sigh from him made her turn back to look at him curiously.

He was smiling a puzzled smile. 'You do confuse me, Nina. Just now I thought you were hurt because you loved him, and then you shock me with a dismissive ''plenty more fish in the sea''. You take the time and effort, to say nothing of the risk, to hitchhike through Europe to find your lover, and then, faced with his impending wedding, you shrug it off.'

Nina stared at him hard and then she stepped towards him, gripped the back of her chair and leaned over him. 'Well, what do you make of that, Mr Lawyer?' she asked thinly, because for sure she couldn't tell him the truth, that the whole damned business was eating away at her insides and everything she said and did was in protection of her emotions.

His eyes were dark and piercing. 'I make quite a lot of it, as it happens. I take your attitude as a warning. You are a tricky lady. I think you have a plan in mind and don't want my suspicions aroused. I think you came here to cause trouble and are now playing it cool. I think I'm going to have to keep a close eye on you while you are here.'

Nina thinned her lips. 'I wonder just how successful a lawyer you are at times,' she goaded. 'You have so little evidence to go on yet already you have me tried and convicted. Well, I take your attitude as a warning, too. You blow as hot and cold as I apparently do. Yes, let's leave Gio out of this for the moment. Let's go back to what happened earlier. That kiss.'

He raised a dark brow and the corner of his mouth twitched and inflamed Nina's senses more.

'Yes, you may well raise your brow,' she hissed at him. 'You came to Palermo to get me because you found out I was making enquiries about Gio Giulianni. So why, Lorenzo Biacci?' Nina cried defiantly. 'Why kiss me that way? Why look at me the way you do at times? Is it all a test? A test to see if I *am* the whore you believe me to be?'

He looked totally dumbstruck for a second, as if he was totally fazed by her accusations. His hand came up and pulled through his hair impatiently, giving him time to think and evaluate what she had just thrown at him.

And Nina waited for his reply, waited with her heart in her mouth, confused too, now, with herself for pushing him this way when his feelings or even thoughts didn't count for anything against the main issue here—her father.

'I couldn't damn well resist you,' he finally scathed at her furiously. 'And, my God, you are right. What the hell does that say about me? To be tempted by a slip of a girl who isn't fit to…to…'

'To what? Clean your boots?' Nina threw at him hotly. 'You damned creep!' she blurted angrily.

'Stop it, Nina!' he ordered thickly. 'This has gone quite far enough!'

'It'll never be far enough for me!' Nina went on heatedly, hands clenched tightly at her sides. 'I find you insufferably arrogant and pompous and—'

He stepped towards her, jerkily, as if to silence her the way he had before. Nina's whole being stiffened and froze and anything further she had been about to verbally fling at him choked in her throat. Her eyes widened fearfully.

And she knew then that all her fury and anger against him was because of one overwhelming thing, and it rocked her senses. His attitude, his thinking the very worst of her, was somehow worse than what she had found out about her father. And it made her head reel to surmise such a thing.

Oh, she was going to have a problem with handling her father's wedding, but she didn't even know the man, had never set eyes on him. But *this* man raging in front of her was flesh and blood, the most exciting, the most infuriating man she had ever met. How hopeless to deny her attraction to him. His very being clawed at her senses. His kiss, his touch, his just standing in front of her set her nerves on edge.

But he thought evil of her and it hurt and she was powerless to do anything about that. If she did blurt the truth, what then? Her father didn't need this on top of his wedding. And she didn't need this feeling rushing inside her, the feelings that this lawyer ignited.

Nina stepped back, almost stumbled out of his reach. 'Please don't,' she implored. 'Don't touch me. Don't say anything! Just leave me alone!'

She turned and fled, then—flew like the wind. Down the terrace steps, across the grass, heading where she didn't know, but at last, breathless and so unbearably hot she could scarcely draw breath, she stopped and gripped the top of a waist-high rough stone wall to steady herself.

Blinking her eyes fiercely, she tried to reign in her confused thoughts but it was impossible. You could only take so much, and this was too much!

'And killing yourself isn't the answer,' she heard, and felt a firm grip on her shoulders.

She was spun around to face the wrath of Lorenzo Biacci. Nina gazed up at him in alarm.

'What do you mean?' she whispered.

Still gripping her firmly, he turned her round to the direction she had been facing before. Nina's eyes widened with horror and then she snapped them tight and almost fell back into Lorenzo's arms with shock.

He held her tightly from behind, his hot body a wall of comfort and protection. Nina had never thought she suffered from vertigo, but now she suspected she did. She felt totally disorientated by what she had just seen. Beyond the rough wall was a perilous drop to craggy rocks on a small cove below and a swollen sea beyond, a drop of hundreds of metres. In her state of sheer anxiety to get away from him she could so easily have toppled over the wall and plunged helplessly to…to…

She drew deep, quick breaths to recover herself, and then all was calm and yet not so calm. His body hard against her back, his arms around her shoulders, the heat of him, the iron-like grip, were new and more fearful dangers.

'I'm all right,' she told him faintly. And then she somehow manoeuvred herself out of his grasp to turn and face him. 'I didn't know…' She smiled nervously, will-power giving her strength. 'I didn't know there was a sheer drop there.' She stepped back, noticing how tense he was, tensed for action if she made any attempt to leap closer to the wall. 'And…and I wasn't thinking of throwing myself over the top,' she told him, shaking her head vigorously. 'No. I'm…I'm not the sort.'

He relaxed slightly, his face grave though. 'Good,' he murmured. 'Better safe than sorry, though.' He took her hand and pulled her back to the path that led to the wall and the shocking drop down to the sea.

Nina pulled her hand back but he simply moved his arm up and around her shoulder. Nina let it stay there because to pull away from him yet again would be a giveaway. He would know that his touch unnerved her, which it did. His touch was fire but she could stand the heat to save face.

Slowly he guided her back through the gardens towards the house. Neither spoke till Nina made the first attempt as they approached the lawned area that stretched towards the terrace. She was calmer now, her mind settled. The grass was strange, thick and broad-bladed beneath her feet, not like thin English grass that grew in English gardens. She mentioned it.

Lorenzo stopped and let her go and Nina stopped too, wondering what she had said.

He was shaking his head again, that puzzled shake of his dark head, as if he couldn't make her out.

'You say the strangest things. What has grass to do with anything?'

Nina tilted her head slightly. 'I was making conversation. I'd have thought that was quite obvious to you.'

'I would say there were plenty of other things we could talk about under the circumstances.'

'Well, the circumstances are rather bizarre,' she cut back, 'and you shouldn't be surprised by anything I say. According to you, I'm a bit of a mystery. A seducer, a troublemaker, and now a potential suicide case. You worry the life out of me, Lorenzo Biacci. If you think my conversation off the wall, listen to yourself now and then.'

She turned her back on him and headed for the terrace steps. He was smiling when he caught up with her.

'The eccentricities of the English,' he murmured.

'The insanity of the Sicilians,' Nina countered, and Lorenzo laughed out loud this time.

They were on the terrace now, still and facing each other. Nina's pulses throbbed disturbingly as she watched his face, alive with humour, more relaxed now. She knew she was in a bigger mess than ever. She wanted to tell him the truth about herself but it was impossible. He might not believe her if she dared to brave it anyway. It was a pretty hopeless situation. So where did they go from here?

She asked. Bluntly and openly. 'So what happens now?'

He looked at her quizzically and then shrugged his shoulders. 'It might be a good idea to finish our lunch.'

'And after?'

His mocking brow rose again, as if she had made an indecent suggestion. Nina passed it off because to rise to it would make her no better than him. She raised her fair brow in defiance of his thoughts, though.

'After, we settle down to quiet domesticity,' he told her as he drew back a chair for her to sit down. 'We are going to have to live together for two and a half weeks and I think there has been enough melodrama for now.'

Nina sat down. 'You have made it all into a melo-drama,' she retorted. 'I'm all for a quiet life.'

'Good, because I have a lot to do before the wedding and I could do without running around after you and dragging you out of trouble every five minutes.'

He reached across the table with the wine bottle and topped up her glass, and this time Nina reached for it unflinchingly. Yes, perhaps a muzzy head was the only way to get through this agony.

Ignoring the fact that he had just spoken to her as if she were five, she lifted the glass of wine aloft. 'OK, truce. Here's to a blissful, uncomplicated existence between us, for however long it takes for you to come to your senses and release me from this prison,' she said caustically. She sipped the wine, noted he didn't raise his glass to acknowledge her toast. So he was getting the message that she had no intentions of making life easy for him. His eyes were narrowed as he gazed at her, still unable to work her out.

Nina smiled as an idea came to her. 'There are terms, of course,' she told him.

Now he took a purposeful mouthful of wine and then replaced the glass on the table. 'I thought there might be,' he muttered ruefully as he twirled the stem of the glass and stared at the fluted crystal as if it was a vessel for foreseeing trouble ahead. 'But no money changes hands till after the wedding.'

Still he thought her the hard-nosed lover, out for what she could make to keep her silence.

'It was never my intention to demand money,' she told him thinly. 'But, seeing as you are so determined to lay some on me, I insist on working for it. You were right. I'm strapped for money and I will need my fare home. I'd intended getting another job in Palermo any-way, bar work or something. But there are no staff here, your housekeeper is away and you say you have work to do, so I can take her place while you get on with it. You know, do the cooking and clean up. Then after this wedding you can pay me and I'll go. I think that's fair, don't you?'

His answer didn't come immediately. Nina watched him with interest. She supposed lawyers weren't renowned for making snap decisions. The odds would have to be weighed. The likelihood of her absconding before the deal was complete had to be considered. Though how he thought she'd get out of this Alcatraz of a place was beyond her. There was his car, though, and the electronic thingy that opened the gates. Seeing as he thought her a 'tricky lady', he'd presume she'd have no trouble stealing those from him in the still of the night.

That was a thought quickly dismissed, though. More than anything else she needed money, and what better way than to stay and earn it? If he agreed.

'What do you think, then?' she urged, getting impatient with waiting for him to come to a decision.

He took a breath. 'Can you cook?'

Nina cheekily gazed at the food set before them. Most of it had simply been assembled rather than cooked—cold meats, shellfish and salad.

'I can,' she told him.

'And cleaning?'

Nina shrugged her shoulders. 'What's a bit of cleaning? A flick of a duster here and there.'

'I'm fastidious about cleanliness. I'm a hard taskmaster to work for.'

'I didn't doubt that you would be,' Nina returned smartly. He could drive her into the ground with his demands but she would do it. She wouldn't give him reason to complain.

'So the domestic arrangements seem to be resolved,'

he said in agreement. 'What do we do about the long hot nights?'

Nina gaped at him. 'W-what long hot nights?'

'The ones that come sandwiched between sundown and sunrise,' he told her flippantly.

And because he went on eating, as if those words hadn't come from his mouth, she ignored them and started eating herself. But it was difficult when her mouth felt as if it was full of cotton wool. The thought of hot Mediterranean nights under the same roof as him was disturbing to say the least. Sure, she could cope with a bit of cooking and housework. The Locastos had put her through the wringer and this place wasn't cluttered with messy, unruly children. No problem. But the long hot nights?

'I shall paint at night,' she told him strongly. 'I'll gather blooms from the garden and do some still lifes in my bedroom, and you can do whatever you do between those hours of sundown and sunrise.'

'I usually spend my nights with a lovely lady whenever the opportunity arises.'

He was winding her up, and confirmation came when the edge of his mouth twitched slightly. Nina was getting used to his ways now.

'How nice for you,' she simpered. 'It's easy to see why you are such a close friend of Gio's, then. You appear to be driven by the same passions. Shame about me, though. I'm a bit more choosy who I spend my nights with and I don't choose *you*.'

Purposefully she forked some more salad onto her plate.

Lorenzo laughed softly under his breath. 'I wasn't actually giving *you* the choice,' he said softly. 'I was just testing the ground to see if you had any objections to my entertaining a girlfriend while you are in residence.'

Nina clenched her fork so tightly she feared it might

bend in her hot hand. Why was she always putting her foot in it with him? He had denied a wife but a girlfriend he hadn't denied. The one whose dress he had given her to wear? She went hot and cold at the thought of him spending hot sultry nights making love to a woman in this lovely old house. She shouldn't feel that way, she had no right, but she felt a throb of jealousy drag at her heart all the same.

She screwed her napkin into a ball, tossed it down on her plate and stood up. 'So long as you don't expect me to cook and clean for her, or them, you can entertain as many women as you please. Now if you'll excuse me I'll get down to my duties.'

She started to pile the plates up. He watched her till her skin burned with embarrassment. He spoke at last, just as she was about to turn away from the table with her arms laden.

'In other words you object very strongly to me bringing a woman here,' he said.

Nina widened her eyes at him. 'I don't remember saying any such thing,' she countered.

'But you feel it.'

Nina let the pile of dirty plates down onto the table again. 'I feel nothing where your love life is concerned,' she told him indignantly. Why was he doing this to her, testing her all the time?

'I think you do. Your cheeks are very pink.'

He stood and caught her arm and pulled her half round the table. His hands were solidly on her shoulders once again. 'I wonder if you go pink all over in the heat of passion?' he murmured softly.

Nina gritted her teeth. 'I don't know; I've never looked,' she told him through tight lips.

'We'll both look next time, then, shall we? It might be fun.'

With that he released her, and she was surprised and

yet not surprised. Slowly but surely she was beginning
to understand the sort of man he was. Heartless. The sort
to use women and then cast them aside like the empty
shell of…of a prawn.

Nina gathered up the empty shells of the prawns as
he turned away and silently entered the house without
looking back. What in heaven's name had she started
when she had found those papers in the bureau? Nothing
but misery and heartache was emerging from it all. Yes,
she had a father, one who wasn't what she'd imagined
at all. He was a man who adored women and used them
and his closest friend was of the same mould. And yet
Lorenzo had said he loved her father as if he were his
own, and to have such feelings for a friend showed a
certain depth of emotion. He couldn't be all bad.

But he thought her bad, and she wasn't free or able
to make him believe otherwise. Not that she wanted to
now. A coldness had come over her when he had suggested bringing a lady-friend home. Of course he would
have hundreds, and when he teased her about passion he
was toying with her feelings, punishing her for being a
mistress.

And she couldn't do anything or say anything to put
it to rights.

She sighed heavily as she carried the plates into the
house and found the kitchen just inside. A huge kitchen
with all modern conveniences.

She put the plates down on the draining board and
looked around the room to get her bearings. The first
thing her eyes settled on was a noticeboard on the wall.
She noticed it because it surprised her. It was covered
in postcards from far-off places and photos, and showed
that Lorenzo Biacci had a human side to him.

One particular photo held her attention. There were
three people in the picture and one was undoubtedly

Lorenzo because it was a recent picture and he looked exactly the same as he did now.

Nina took it down and held it in cold, trembling fingers. The girl at his side was beautiful, dark and sultry and was clinging possessively to Lorenzo's arm. The man behind was older and had his arms around them both. Nina stared at it hard, striving to find something that would suggest that the older man might be her father. He was dark, too, but with distinguished grey at his temples. He was very good-looking, younger than Nina had imagined her father to be, and she went to put it back because she was almost sure the man couldn't be Gio. There was no family resemblance whatsoever to her.

'You can keep it if you want to. It's the closest you'll get to him this time. The girl beside me is his daughter, so now you know something perhaps you didn't know before, and perhaps it will help you to realise how mismatched the two of you were. There can't be more than a year or two's difference in Gio's daughter's age and your own.'

Nina swung around and faced Lorenzo, her face pinched with pain, her heart still as a bottomless lake. Her head swam and her eyes blurred over so that she couldn't see his face clearly. But the tone of his voice was enough for Nina. Cold and censorious, as if he was speaking to the lowest form of human life.

The photo fluttered from her fingers and she moved towards the door. Somehow she found her way upstairs and along the corridor to her bedroom, and she stood for a very long time with her stiffened back against the door and her eyes squeezed tightly shut.

She had a sister, and that man behind her and Lorenzo in the photo *was* her father. And…and the daughter, her half-sister, looked besotted with Lorenzo Biacci. Was she the girlfriend Lorenzo had asked if she objected to bringing to the house? Nina's head swam till she wanted to scream with the pain of it all.

She shouldn't have come. Oh, God, she shouldn't have come to Sicily. She didn't want to be here. It was hurting now and there would surely be more to come. She wouldn't be able to bear it.

CHAPTER FIVE

'NINA, this has gone far enough. Twice a day is obsessional. And besides, sight of your pert little rear presented so delectably in those skimpy shorts while you are on your hands and knees is not doing my blood pressure a lot of good.'

'You shouldn't have high blood pressure at your age,' Nina huffed as she polished away for all her worth. Twice a day on her hands and knees was sort of obsessional, she guessed, but it worked wonders for the mind and spirit to say nothing of the waistline. She was certainly taking her duties seriously.

She paused for breath and sat back on her heels, turning the polishing cloth around in her hands. She looked up at him leaning in the kitchen doorway, all nonchalant coolness in linen chinos and a mulberry-coloured silk shirt with the sleeves rolled back. He was barefoot, too, which amused Nina. First sight of him had been his shiny crocodile shoes. At that moment of acknowledging his cool sophistication she wouldn't have imagined him padding around barefoot.

She smiled. It was all right when it was like this—normal, him lightly teasing her, she quick to give him a snappy retort. The rest, though? It puzzled her as she seemed to puzzle him. So many times since coming here she'd caught him eyeing her with what could only be described as broody thoughtfulness. Not sure of her and yet seemingly not wanting to understand her.

She supposed she was a mystery to him. Here she was, supposedly the ex-mistress of Gio Giulianni, a wealthy, successful man, on her hands and knees polishing the tiled kitchen floor till it shone enough to see your reflection in it.

'It's Carlo that makes all the mess,' she told him. 'Hair all over the place and his dusty paw-marks. It needs doing twice a day.'

His dark brows rose slightly. 'And whose fault is that? He's not usually allowed in the house, you know. When you leave I'll have some explaining to do.'

'I'll tell Carlo before I go. He'll understand.' She bent over and started vigorously rubbing the floor again, the thought of leaving this wonderful place tightening her stomach. She loved it here, would have scrubbed to eternity and back to be able to stay here for the rest of her life. She loved the cool old house with its sombre, elegant tranquillity but when you stepped outside the vibrancy and flamboyance of the tropical gardens hit you and made your blood sing. And still *he* made her blood sing, and she suspected that if she stayed much longer she might need a blood transfusion in the not too distant future.

She was suddenly scooped up from the floor and her polishing cloth plucked from her fingers to land on the top of the fridge.

Lorenzo held her firmly by her waist and his eyes gleamed with a sudden intensity that had her blood rushing once again. Because of the way he was holding her she was forced to rest her own hands on his arms. Very intimate and disconcerting.

'I wasn't intending to explain anything to the dog. I meant my housekeeper,' he said gruffly.

Nina widened her eyes teasingly. 'Yes, but you'll have to explain to Carlo first. It's only fair.'

He smiled in hopeless resignation. 'Nina,' he breathed, 'you are impossible.' Then his eyes changed from light to dark, a sure sign of his change of mood. 'Where did you meet him?' he asked softly.

'Why, out there on the terrace, of course. You were there. Kissing me, if I remember rightly.'

His hands tightened and pressed into her small waist. His eyes were dark and broody again. 'Why do you do this all the time? Take verbal evasive action when I mention Gio?'

Yes, she did it all the time. It was the only way. She'd known he was referring to Gio and acting dumb had seemed to be the simplest way out of a tricky situation. After finding the photograph of the happy threesome she didn't want chapter and verse on their lives. The photograph was reinstated back on the noticeboard and Nina, in quiet moments when Lorenzo was working and she was cooking, would take surreptitious glances at it.

She was past the stage of staring at her father's image with curiosity. A photo was simply an image, no insight into the man himself in spite of the old cliché that every picture tells a story. But time and time again her eyes would settle on Lorenzo and the face of the dark, sultry girl who was her half-sister. Now there was a story, one she didn't want to hear. Her defences were up, good and strong, where that scenario was concerned. But she was even past the stage of staring at *her* in avid curiosity and wondering about their relationship. It was Lorenzo who held her attention and close scrutiny because he was real. The here and now. The one image out of the three that was flesh and blood to her. Like at this very instant, holding her, imprinting his masculinity and sexuality on her very soul.

As a fail-safe she stepped back from him to break their physical contact and bent to pick up the plastic container of liquid wax polish from the floor. 'Why do you keep bringing him up?' she countered. 'You have succeeded in keeping me out of his way and you should be grateful I'm not giving you any hassle over him. End of story, really.'

'It's not as simple as that, though, is it?'

She crossed the room to retrieve the polishing cloth from the fridge and with the polish put it away in the cleaning cupboard.

'It is, though. Very simple. Gio is getting married and there is nothing I can do or say about the matter.'

'You came all this way to Sicily to find him, put yourself through all sorts of traumas and now you have given up on him?'

'It's what you want. It's the sensible thing to do, isn't it?'

She turned to face him, to challenge him. Whatever did he think she was likely to do under the circumstances? The circumstances he had created for her.

'I don't know what I did expect you to do, come to think of it,' he said thoughtfully. 'Certainly not to get down on your knees every five minutes scrubbing for the Olympics.'

'They were the terms of our agreement,' she reminded him. 'I would forget Gio and work for you, and then after the wedding you would pay me and I'd be on the first flight home. Thank you and goodbye, Nina Parker.'

'You see, you are doing it again.'

'What?'

'Putting on a brave face,' he said quietly as he leaned back against the work surface.

She smiled. 'It's what rejected mistresses do, or should do if they are in their right minds.' She *supposed*. Not having ever been a mistress, she was at a loss as to how one might act faced with losing a lover.

'Very sensible of you, but a bit out of character, surely?'

'Oh, dear,' she sighed wearily. 'Is that a statement or a question? If it's a question it means I have to answer it, and it's far too hot for me to try analysing myself.'

She brushed the hair from her forehead, longing to be

outside as another hot afternoon laboured towards a
slightly cooler evening. She didn't like it when he
brought Gio into the conversation because she was so
afraid of giving herself away, and that would certainly
complicate matters more than they already were.

Now there was a legitimate daughter of Gio's she
hadn't known about, and, though she had anticipated that
he might have a family, coming face to face with her
photograph wasn't as easy to cope with as she would
have liked. And though she was curious to know about
his previous marriage to that lovely girl's mother, and
now this pending wedding to another woman, letting
sleeping dogs lie would be a very apt course of action
in this case. Nina just didn't want to know.

'Take it as a statement, then,' Lorenzo decided. 'My
analysis of you. A feisty young woman tripping from
one disaster to another and yet acting extremely sensibly
when faced with her lover about to be married to another
woman. Something doesn't ring true.'

Nina shrugged. Perhaps she should have thrown a few
wobblies, cried herself into the night, making sure he
heard, and wandered around tearing at her hair like a
lost, tormented soul. Maybe that was the way rejected
mistresses *did* act.

'Ah, but I haven't come face to face with him, have
I?' she countered.

'Would you feel differently if you did? Would it re-
kindle burning passions of the past?' he asked sombrely.

Nina gave him a sweet smile of contempt. 'You mean
would I realise what I was missing—his wealth—and
once again go for the jugular of his bank account?' she
stated sarcastically.

Lorenzo shook his head. 'I didn't mean that at all.'

Nina jutted her chin. 'I think you did. You think I'm
out for the main chance; you always have done. A
younger woman and an older man having an affair. To

you it can only mean something unsavoury and merce-
nary.'

'And it was moonlight and roses all the way, was it?'

Nina sneered at his cynicism. 'Stop it, Lorenzo, you're
beginning to sound like a detective.'

'And still you take evasive action when I try and find
out more about your affair with Gio.'

Nina's eyes widened. 'Lorenzo Biacci,' she said, and
exhaled. 'It is none of your business!'

'I'm curious.' He shrugged.

'Curious or jealous?' she snapped without thinking.

As soon as the accusation was out Nina wanted to
suck it back in through her teeth, because of course the
very idea was absurd. But when he didn't respond with
a splutter of denial, or at the very least a laugh of derision, she began to wonder. And the conjecture had her
heart thudding dizzily. Was he jealous of her supposed
affair with Gio? So many times he brought Gio into the
conversation, probing for answers she was unable to give
him because it had never happened, and she was wary
of saying anything that would give her secret away. But
to be jealous you had to have feelings to warrant that
jealousy. Feelings for her? It was an exciting thought
but one she dismissed quickly and sensibly.

'Let's take a bottle of wine outside. You paint and I'll
watch,' he suggested, as if she had never spoken.

Nina stared at the back of his head as he reached
inside the fridge for a bottle of white wine. How very
interesting. No denial and yet no admittance that she was
right and he was wild with jealousy. But what on earth
had she expected? Neither, actually, because the suggestion was absurd and he had treated it accordingly. It
was too silly to warrant an answer or even a comment.

'You know I make mistakes when you are breathing
down my neck all the time,' she protested feebly. Apart
from putting her paintbrush in the wrong place when he

was watching her work, she found her heart all over the place, too, when he leaned so close. It was very off-putting.

He swung round from the fridge. 'I'm flattered,' he said, with a knowing smile that brought colour to Nina's face.

He's just a flirt, Nina reminded herself. She turned away from him to gather up her sketchpad and water-colours, which she kept on a big old dresser in the kitchen. Hopeless to protest that she would rather work alone. Lorenzo did as he pleased and would join her anyway.

Usually she painted after lunch—found a shady spot in the garden and dabbled to her heart's content. Carlo always joined her; stretched out in the same shady spot, he'd snore to keep her company. She wasn't used to taking a siesta, hadn't been brought up with it, but Lorenzo was and he rested for an hour or so in the cool of the house. He worked all morning and emerged from his air-conditioned study for the light lunch she always had waiting for him, then he would disappear to his suite of rooms upstairs.

Later he would find her in the garden and watch her paint. By now Carlo was getting a little more used to Lorenzo, and only growled half-heartedly when he leaned too close to Nina to see how progress on her work was going. All the same, it had the desired effect. Not once had Lorenzo tried to become too intimate with her during those painting sessions.

'Look, we'll take this tray and pile everything on it,' she suggested, reaching for one down by the side of a unit. She took the wine from his hands and put it on the tray and then took glasses from a cupboard above his head. She filled an empty mineral water bottle from the tap and took a dish to wash her brushes in. 'There, I think that's everything.'

She picked up the tray and lifted her head to see his dark brooding eyes eating her up again. Her heart somersaulted. She wished he wouldn't do that—watch her so intently. It gave her goose-bumps.

He took the tray from her hands. 'I'll take that,' he said, and his voice was curiously thick.

Nina followed him out of the kitchen and blinked in the bright sunlight, glad to be out in the air. She didn't know how long she could stand all this—him staring at her all the time. It was a relief when he wasn't around and yet she missed his presence when he wasn't. It was a curious state of affairs. She knew her heart was in danger, though. He was so attractive, evermore so the longer she stayed.

She enjoyed cooking for him, enjoyed his appreciation of her efforts, and oddly she got enormous pleasure from the mundane housework, though polishing antique furniture was hardly mundane; it was more a voyage of discovery for her artistic mind. She loved handling beautiful objects, turning ancient, ornate Italian glassware in her hands and feeling the history it held and wondering what sights it had seen in its time.

Lorenzo had laughed lightly but not derisively when one evening she had admitted to him how she felt about his collection of antique vases displayed in the long sitting room. He found it amusing that she thought inanimate objects, beautiful as they were, to have minds and souls. She had laughed and said she wasn't quite mad yet, and that wasn't exactly what she'd meant, and the conversation had progressed to Lorenzo telling her more about the history of his family heirlooms.

But listening to him, enjoyable though it was, left Nina feeling that curious void in her own life again. She had no background, no family heirlooms, no history, and it saddened her deeply though she didn't show it. It was only when she lay in bed at night, ears alerted to the slightest sound—the cicadas buzzing outside, the slight rush of wind in the poplars on the edge of the estate— that she allowed that sad, empty feeling to claim her fully.

Because of Gio Giulianni she was part Sicilian and she longed to know more, to feel part of a real family. Whatever the man was—how could she judge without meeting him?—he was still her natural father. And she had a half-sister, and that damned photograph of her clinging to Lorenzo haunted her. Were they romantically involved? Did she want to know if they were? Was her resolve to let sleeping dogs lie slipping away from her?

'Tell me about Gio's daughter,' she said as, side by side, they went down the terrace steps. She held her breath, inwardly cursing herself for being so weak in asking.

'What brought that on?' Lorenzo asked as he shifted the tray to one arm and reached out his free hand to assist her on the last couple of steps which had crumbled with age.

Nina took his arm and leapt them, landing ahead of him and letting go of his arm. She stopped to adjust the heel of her downtrodden espadrilles. Lorenzo waited, eyeing her curiously.

Nina shrugged and smiled to hide her regret for asking. She really didn't want to know, and yet part of her ached to know *something*. Perhaps he would be discreet enough to tell her only what she wanted to know, but it was silly, really; he couldn't possibly know just what she wanted to hear.

'I'm curious,' she mimicked.

Lorenzo smiled and turned away. 'Or jealous because she was hanging onto my arm so intimately in the photo?'

She'd asked for that. She walked beside him, kicking stray pebbles from the path that led to the gardens.

'To be jealous I'd have to care in the first place and I don't,' she told him rather shortly.

'I'm disappointed. I was beginning to think you rather liked me.'

He was teasing, not taking her seriously, and it was the best possible way to find out more without getting in too deeply.

'I do rather like you,' she admitted. 'You are a bit peculiar but I don't hold that against you. You could be making my life a misery but you're not.'

They had reached the spot where Nina usually painted. A stone seat sat against a hedge of hibiscus in the corner of a sheltered rose garden. All around the seat there were terracotta pots crammed with huge-headed vermillion geraniums that Nina painted avidly. Nina stopped and waited for him to go on, expecting him to tell her about Gio's daughter.

'Not here,' Lorenzo said. 'You've done those pots to death. Have you discovered the pantheon yet?'

'The pantheon?'

'Obviously not. Follow me.'

Nina sighed as she did as she was bid. It was all right for him to ask probing questions about her affair with Gio, but when she asked intimate questions he was completely unforthcoming. No doubt because he didn't trust her enough, thinking she might use the information in some adverse way. Or because he was romantically involved with Gio's daughter and it was none of her business. Whatever, she sensed she wasn't going to get anything out of him but another session of him breathing down her neck and putting her off her work.

Nina thought she had explored every secret niche of his wondrous garden, but when he pushed through an overgrown clump of waist-high wild rosemary and thorny gorse she realised she had missed this bit.

'It's not *the* pantheon, of course,' he told her over his

shoulder as he took a winding path down to a shady glade.

'I didn't think for a minute it was,' she laughed.

He nodded to her to open a scrolled wrought-iron gate set in a wall of grey stone because his hands were full with the tray.

Nina could already see through the gate, and what met her eyes was quite astonishing. Hesitantly she pushed it open, and it let out a grinding plea for maintenance.

'This gate needs some oil,' she said as she heaved her weight against it.

Lorenzo laughed softly again, and Nina turned to him and looked shamefaced. Her voice was a whisper when she spoke. 'Sorry, that sounded crass. Are your family buried here?'

Lorenzo had to put the tray down on a curved stone bench-seat inside the garden for fear of dropping it as he laughed out loud. 'Heaven forbid. My mother would find that very amusing. No, this isn't a mausoleum; it's my mother's temple to the gods. When she's here she collects sculptures and stone statues of the gods, as you can see.'

And Nina did indeed feast her eyes—on the most incredible collection of marble and stone statues she had seen outside the British Museum. The secret walled garden was much bigger than she had thought from the other side of the gate. Inside the garden she could now see leafy walkways and lovely old stone seats where you could rest and think. Each delightful statue was set amongst wispy foliage and small shrubs: lavender and wild thyme and cultivated rosemary and sage. The herby scents were overwhelmingly strong after the heat of the day; they actually swam in your head. Nina felt quite overcome with the effect of it all. Because it was Sicily, and hot and sunny, the garden wasn't at all spooky, but she thought it might have been if it had been set in a cold, wet climate.

'They're lovely,' Nina sighed. 'The whole garden is so...so peaceful and restful.' She sat on her hands on the stone seat next to the tray and breathed the fragrant air. 'I think I would like your mother if I ever met her,' she said.

Lorenzo's head jerked up from the bottle of wine he was about to open. 'I doubt that,' he muttered.

Nina glanced at him quickly. It was a strange remark to make, and then she suddenly realised why he had said it. It was a very pushy thing to say—that she would like his mother if she met her. It was almost hinting at an intimate relationship with him. She swallowed quickly and looked away from him, gazed down a walkway where naked stone-faced lovers embraced, arms entwined, their bodies almost writhing against each other. She shivered then, because she felt a little strange inside. Some of the statues were erotic, and she couldn't help making a comparison with flesh and blood. The nearest to hand, Lorenzo Biacci. She bit her lip and her wide grey eyes searched for a less revealing statue she could fix her gaze on and get her head together.

'Wine.'

Nina took the glass he offered and hoped her hand didn't shake. She was about to ask if his mother would mind if she sketched some of the figures but quickly changed her mind. That would sound pushy, too, and besides she might get an answer that would put her firmly in her place, like, Why should she? You're not likely to meet her anyway.

'So,' Nina bravely started after taking a sip of wine and putting the glass down on the ground beside her, 'What shall I paint today? Oh, no, we forgot Carlo!' she suddenly exclaimed, and went to get up. 'I always let him out at this time and he loves to watch me paint and he…'

She didn't finish. Lorenzo reached out and stopped her.

'Not here.'

His eyes locked with hers so meaningfully she read him loud and clear. Carlo wasn't wanted here because the huge, silly dog wouldn't allow Lorenzo Biacci near her. The secret garden was walled, totally secluded, heady with perfume, damned erotic in fact, and Lorenzo's eyes were eating her up again and his fingers were seductively stroking the inside of her palm. Her eyes widened and her blood shooshed dramatically.

'OK, let's get down to it… I mean… Oh, what do I mean? I mean what shall I draw first?' Nina asked.

'How about my mouth?' Lorenzo suddenly breathed, and before she knew what had happened Lorenzo had leaned across the curved bench and taken her own quivering lips in a very firm, meaningful kiss that quickly developed into a softer, more erotic sort.

His mouth was so sensual, such a sweet temptation in this garden of Eden where even the stone statues seemed to have hearts and souls. Her head swam, the sweet smell of herbs seeming to act as an aphrodisiac to her senses. It was the most perfect place on earth for seduction and she was in the arms of the most perfect person on earth created for seduction. How easily she could drift and let it happen, let him love her till she turned to stone and was immortalised for evermore.

At last he drew back from her, and she blinked open her drowsy eyes and thought perhaps some mythical god had in fact turned her to stone as a punishment for enjoying that so much. Her body had indeed frozen, with the surprise of his lips on hers, but inside she was molten gold, hot and smouldering.

'Your eyes are all sparkly,' he murmured as he lifted

his hand to smooth his thumb across the soft curve of her chin.

'Are they?' she murmured back, wondering what to add to that to break this spell she was caught up in. But there was nothing to draw on, no inspiration for some witty retort to break this paralysis that was binding her body so tightly.

'May I paint them?'

Nina's eyes widened till they hurt. 'P-paint them?' she uttered feebly.

'And the rest,' he murmured, and leaned forward to plant a very soft kiss on the tip of her nose.

Confusion swept her, and wide-eyed she watched as he picked up her sketchpad and flicked the pages over to a fresh, clean sheet. He opened her case of water-colours, poured some of the water into the dish and sorted through her bundle of brushes till he found one that suited him.

Nina's mouth finally worked. 'You paint? You never said.' She was quite astonished because when he had watched her working he'd usually asked the sort of naive questions that indicated he knew nothing about art.

'You never asked,' he murmured, without looking at her. He was busy mixing burnt sienna and white from a separate pot she carried.

'But you asked all sorts of silly questions, like why did I use so much blue in my shading.'

'Only because everyone has different ways of doing things, and I was curious as to what you see and I don't. I tend to use grey for my shading because that is the colour I see shadows. The world is seen differently through the eye of every viewer but basically it's all the same, our perception is different, that's all. That is why no two pictures can ever be the same. Don't you agree?'

Nina opened and shut her mouth, quite speechless.

He looked up at her astonished face and smiled. 'What's wrong? Don't you agree?'

Nina found her voice. She managed a small laugh too. 'I'm just surprised, that's all. I didn't think you had any talent in that way—you know, artistic talent.' Gosh, if she had known she would have made more mistakes than ever over her work. His very presence watching her paint had put her off, it would have been worse knowing he was a talented artist too.

She laughed suddenly. 'Ah, but now I'm taking it for granted that you have some talent. You might be quite hopeless.'

'Yes, I might be, but you can be the judge of that when I've finished. Now, no peeking.' He lifted his dark head and nodded to a stone seat across from them. 'Over there. I can see you better and, besides, you sitting so close puts temptation in my way.'

Nina was up like a shot, smoothing her T-shirt down over her hips. Was she a temptation to him? Or was he just teasing again? She didn't question it anyway, and moved over to the other seat where the head of Minerva on a stone plinth watched over her. Yes, best she was over here and not right on top of him.

She sat in silence, but her thoughts went wild in her head. The things he said and the way he said them, the looks he gave her. She had chosen to block it all out because it was so scary.

She sucked in her lower lip and fixed her gaze on him. He tutted, and she released her lip but didn't take her gaze from him. Face facts, she told herself. They were strongly attracted to each other but so far an on-looker would never know. They had covered it, buried it, swept it under the rug of their seemingly innocent domestic routine. But if either of them snapped it could only mean trouble. It would be a dreadful complication if anything happened between them. One she could hardly bear to think about.

Lorenzo was very much embroiled in Gio's life but not completely in his confidence, as he had stated. She, Nina Parker, was the proof of that. Lorenzo knew nothing about Gio's illegitimate daughter, and for her to get emotionally involved with him would be too dangerous. Lorenzo had said that this Sofia was right for him and they should have been married years ago. Something had obviously prevented that happening sooner and it sounded as if any more waves in their lives might alter things.

What had Lorenzo meant about Gio's dark past? Was that lovely girl, her half-sister, somehow a part of that dark, mysterious past?

And would she be any the wiser by the time she left? It saddened her to think she was so close to her father and was not able to meet him. Even just to wish him well for his future without divulging who she was would give her a small measure of comfort.

She sighed, and Lorenzo tutted again. She tried to relax but it was almost impossible. She tried to put everything from her mind but that was near impossible too. She was gazing at a man who was seriously beginning to matter in her life but it was all hopeless. For everyone's sake she couldn't afford to let her heart fly free with Lorenzo. Eventually she would have to leave Sicily, and it wasn't a good feeling at all. She had arrived here with such high hopes of meeting her real father but those hopes were dashed now. More than likely she would leave Sicily with a broken heart, because the more she thought about Lorenzo Biacci the more she thought he would be the breaker of it.

'Hey, why so stern? Relax, Nina.'

Nina smiled. 'I hope you are flattering me. I've been

watching your brushstrokes and they are whizzing over the paper. Are you sure you know what you are doing?'

Actually, she strongly suspected he was doing a caricature of her, because she was hardly sitting in an elegant pose. She had simply plonked herself down on the seat and clutched her hands tightly in her lap. She was bolt-upright as well, not relaxed at all, and hardly fluid enough for him to do a flattering picture of her.

'I know exactly what I am doing,' he reassured her. 'After all I had an excellent tutor when I was younger.'

'Oh, yes, who was that? Leonardo da Vinci?' she teased.

He smiled thinly. 'Gio, of course. You must know how talented an artist he is?'

Lorenzo's words spun around the top of her head like a raging tornado. She thought she might fall off the stone seat any second. Heat flooded her and it was nothing to do with the sun overhead, the pungent scent of herbs, or even the stone gods creating a storm on her senses.

How often had she dreamed that she had got her own talent from her father? How often had she wondered? She had confirmation now, but instead of filling her vacuum with happiness it sucked at her very bones. Gio was an artist; she had his genes. They could be so close, bonded by their talent and artistic flair, but it wasn't to be. It couldn't be.

'But then perhaps you didn't know,' Lorenzo said darkly as she made no effort to speak a word of acceptance or denial. 'Perhaps you were so physically attracted to each other anything aesthetic didn't come into your hot affair,' he added.

His tone was icy cold and Nina's stomach clenched and her jawline stiffened. She couldn't take that—no, not that awful, sordid accusation. Shakily she got to her feet and narrowed her eyes at him. Suddenly the garden was crowding her, the scent of herbs suffocating her, the damned statues mocking her.

'That remark was completely uncalled for,' she said through tight lips. 'I wonder if you would have dared to have spoken it to Gio himself? I think not. Yet you feel able to deliver it to me with that cynically icy tone of yours because I'm not a man, just a mere mistress who in your eyes isn't afforded any respect. Well, damn you, Lorenzo Biacci. For your attitude, for your arrogance, for just about everything!'

She had to cross the mossy patch of green to get to the gate and her escape but Lorenzo barred her way, caught her arm and swung her around until she was flat up against his broad chest.

His breath was hot on her cheek as he rasped out. 'I apologise. Do you recognise an apology when you hear one?' he challenged angrily. 'I wish I could take the words back but it's too late; they have been delivered and I'm sorry. If you took the time and the trouble to think about what I said you'd know the reason why I said it.'

'Well, I'm not a mind-reader,' she cried, equally angrily, angry at that insult and doubly so at his anger at her reaction to it. 'And I'm just working on what I know to date about you, your obsession with me and Gio—'

'Yes, eating me up inside, Nina,' he growled at her. 'Damned well eating me up inside, because I want you for myself and—'

Suddenly he let her go, as if she were highly explosive and unsafe to handle, in a white-hot rage.

Nina stepped back with shock, her hands clenched so tightly at her sides her nails were threatening to draw blood from her palms. He *was* jealous.

And she didn't know what to say or how to act or what to think. Nothing in life had ever prepared her for being wanted by such a charismatic man. She was ordinary Nina Parker who had come to seek her roots, and now…now she was a mistress…now she was enraging the most exciting man she had ever met and she didn't know how to handle it now that it was out in the open.

She took long breaths as their eyes warred with each other. He said nothing more, just ate her up with those dark brooding eyes, silently urging her to say or do something.

She turned away because suddenly she couldn't breathe any more. She went to grab at her paints and brushes and sketchpad, and then she took a sharp intake of breath at the sheet Lorenzo had been working on.

Her fingers trembled violently as she lifted the pad from the stone seat. Her eyes widened fearfully as she gazed at it.

No caricature met her wide grey eyes, simply the most beautiful, the most…oh, God, she was lost for words. It was nothing like she had expected, no amusing carica-ture. It was her, though. Nina Parker. But not the Nina Parker who had sat stiffly on a stone seat with Minerva breathing down her neck.

It was her on the first day she had arrived here, sprawled naked on a soft, downy bed of silk, head to one side with her long blonde hair fanned across the pillow, completely and utterly at peace with the world. And yet each stroke of his sepia-tinted brush seemed to draw out every erotic curve of her body. She might have been sound asleep, having no knowledge of his presence, but her whole form seemed to be crying out for him. Arms flung out, her small hands slightly curved, almost beckoning him down to her, long brown legs slightly apart, inviting, that small Mona Lisa smile on her moist lips.

Oh, no, that wasn't her, not the real Nina Parker.

She swung round and glared at Lorenzo, who was watching her, waiting for her to say something. And what could she say? What had life ever taught her to prepare herself for this? It was the most beautiful, the most erotic picture she had ever seen, and it was her. Her and yet not her.

He seemed to bore into her very thinking, to scour out her most intimate thoughts and spring them to the surface.

'That's the way I see you, Nina. The way I want you as much as you want me,' he breathed throatily.

She wanted to toss a throwaway remark at him but nothing came from the defences within her. Instead her eyes filled with tears because she knew something he didn't: that wanting wasn't enough and wanting wasn't possible anyway. There was too much at stake, too many people's emotions to protect. Her father's for one. He was about to be married and she would be a shock. And his daughter—she didn't even know her name—her feelings had to be considered. And Sofia, whoever she was, the bride-to-be who had waited so long. None of them had asked for an illegitimate daughter to be thrown at them.

And Lorenzo? He could live with not having it happen for him. She was simply someone ephemeral in his life—here today and gone tomorrow. And as for her own feelings... What was new in her life? You couldn't miss something you had never had. She had never felt as if she belonged to someone, body and soul.

Blinking away the tears, she left everything as it was on the curved stone seat and left him alone in the scented garden with the statues for company.

CHAPTER SIX

'COME on, Carlo, don't sulk,' Nina pleaded as she unbolted his run.

He was usually at the wire mesh waiting for her, hearing her steps from way off. It was the first place she had thought to come after leaving Lorenzo fuming in the garden. She needed to be far away from him, to collect her thoughts, to repress everything he had said and made her feel. The picture had shocked her, he had shocked her, but she was calming down now. It was all impossible and she had to put it behind her. Later she would have to think about it, though. She couldn't stay any longer, not now. She had to leave.

She crossed the grassed area, nervously gabbling to Carlo as she approached his kennel. 'Yes, I did momentarily forget you, but then Lorenzo said you weren't allowed in the secret garden and he had a point.' She shrugged. 'You wouldn't have liked it anyway. It's a spooky place. I didn't think so at first, but then it got all sort of shadowy and gloomy. You didn't miss anything.'

Carlo was having none of her excuses. He lay in his kennel, his head lolling out of the open door, panting slightly.

Nina crouched down beside him with sudden concern. 'Hey, fella, what's wrong?' And something *was* wrong, she sensed. He was hot, unnaturally so; she could feel the backs of his ears burning through the thick coat of hair.

Nina pulled at his collar to try and get him to his feet and drag him out into his run, so she could take a closer look at him. Carlo helped her, tried to get to his feet,

101

but only managed to sidle his way out into the open on his belly.

Nina saw the problem straight away. His front left paw was swollen alarmingly. Early this morning she had taken him for a run down to the cliff edge and along the wall for a kilometre or so. The land had been rough and uncultivated and Carlo had raced like the wind, but she had seen no sign that he had injured himself.

Now she saw the problem. The pad was hot and swollen with infection and she suspected it was cut.

'Come on, darling,' she encouraged, hiding her concern from him. 'Make an effort to get up because I haven't the strength to carry you to the house.'

Carlo obeyed reluctantly and managed to get up onto three legs. The hurt paw hung loosely in front of him and his eyes looked so pained and sad Nina wanted to cry for him.

With Carlo limping slowly behind her, and Nina giving him encouraging sounds, it still took for ever to get back to the house. With a sigh of relief Nina saw Lorenzo standing on the terrace gazing out over the gardens, deep in thought, not seeing her and Carlo approaching.

All thoughts of the afternoon and Lorenzo's burning insult faded from Nina's thinking with the urgency of Carlo's suffering. She called out to Lorenzo and waved her hand at him.

'Carlo is hurt,' she cried out.

Lorenzo was with her in a second, bending down to Carlo, who had collapsed with exhaustion at Nina's heels, panting laboriously in the heat of the sun and the effort of trying to walk in pain.

'That's a bad infection,' Lorenzo stated worriedly.

'Is there a vet nearby?' Nina asked hopefully, and then dashed the thought. They were a million miles from anywhere.

'I think we can deal with this ourselves,' Lorenzo said, taking a closer look at the infected paw. 'I think he has something in it—a thorn or a piece of glass.'

'He was all right this morning,' Nina told him, on her knees next to him.

'Infection sets in quickly in the heat. Come on, Carlo, old boy, let's give you a hand.'

Nina leapt to her feet as Lorenzo effortlessly scooped the huge dog up into his arms. Carlo let out one snarl of protest and then sensibly shut up as Lorenzo carried him to the terrace and into the kitchen.

Nina ran to one of the tall cupboards in the utility area of the kitchen and pulled out an old travel blanket she had seen stored there. She laid it on the floor by the open door and Lorenzo gently lowered Carlo onto it.

'Hold his head while I take a closer look,' he ordered Nina.

Nina sat cross-legged on the floor and held Carlo's head in her lap, ready to clamp her hands over his jaws if he made any attempt to snap at Lorenzo. The weakened dog stared at her wide-eyed and Nina grinned down at him.

'It's for your own good, Carlo. Lorenzo won't hurt you, I promise you.' She stroked his ears soothingly.

'It looks like a thorn,' Lorenzo said gravely, 'a big one, and very deeply embedded and infected. It'll have to come out.'

'Where are you going?' she asked worriedly as Lorenzo got up and left the room. Perhaps there *was* a local vet he could call up. It must be more serious than he had first thought.

'I've a scalpel in my study. I use it for trimming photographs. Could you boil some water while I get it?'

Shakily Nina got up and put a pan of water on the stove. A scalpel? Lorenzo was going to do it himself. Much as she adored Carlo and he adored her, she would have been very wary if taking on the task herself. A dog in pain wasn't to be taken lightly, and he and Lorenzo were hardly the best of friends.

Suddenly the weight of her own responsibility hit her. She would be up at the dangerous end, ready to restrain a pair of lethal jaws from Lorenzo's throat if Lorenzo hurt him during the operation. She didn't fear for herself, but would she be able to control the dog if he took a lunge at Lorenzo?

She gulped as Lorenzo came back into the room with a first aid box and the fine-bladed scalpel.

'Are you sure you want to do this, Lorenzo?' she whispered. 'An animal in pain can be fearsome.'

Lorenzo smiled to reassure her. 'I have no choice. I couldn't bear the wrath of you or my housekeeper if anything happened to him. Besides, I'm not the bastard you think me to be. I do have a heart, Nina.'

'Well, you're going to need more than a heart; you're going to need nerves of steel to do what you're going to do,' Nina bit out at him, already tense herself at the thought of what he was going to have to do.

'Oh, I have them in abundance, too,' he told her cynically as he opened the first aid box and sorted through it, looking for things he might need. 'And patience by the bucket load,' he added. 'I've had to use the lot since picking you up from the back streets of Palermo.'

Nina sighed. He was still angry with her, and that wasn't altogether fair, but this wasn't the right moment for them to be snapping at each other.

'OK, this isn't the time to argue, Lorenzo. I'm sorry, too, for what it's worth, but your insensitive remark earlier really got to me, and then seeing that picture you did of me—well, that got to me, too. I'm not like that—not one bit. All wanton and wanting... You painted me as if I was—'

He wasn't even listening. Concern for Carlo was furrowing his brow. Nina bit her lip and turned back to the steaming pan of water. She took a dish from the cupboard and poured the boiling water in it.

Together they crouched over Carlo, Lorenzo holding his injured paw firmly but tenderly as he examined it in more detail. Nina shifted her position to hold Carlo's head in her lap, stroking his ears and leaning close to him to soothe him with her soft voice.

'Oh,' Nina murmured after a while, gazing down at Carlo, 'he's sound asleep.' She smiled through her tears of concern for the big soft dog. 'Oh, Lorenzo, he's snoring.'

Lorenzo smiled at her and held up the offending thorn between his finger and thumb.

'Oh, you've done it!' she cried. Her eyes shot to Carlo's paw and it was all neatly bound in clean white bandage. And Carlo was resting peacefully. 'Oh, Lorenzo,' she breathed in relief, 'you're wonderful.'

She laid Carlo's head down on the blanket and leapt to her feet as Lorenzo got to his. She did the first thing that occurred to her—flung her arms around Lorenzo's neck and hugged him tightly.

'Oh, you were wonderful. You didn't hurt him at all and now he will love you for ever.'

'And you know what that means.' Lorenzo laughed softly in her ear.

Nina leapt back, flushing hotly and laughing nervously, and sniffing and crying all at the same time. Her eyes blinked feverishly. Yes, Carlo would no longer see Lorenzo as a threat to her.

Lorenzo shook his head at the apprehension on her face, but he was smiling as he handed her the silk handkerchief he took from his pocket.

'Wipe your tears away,' he told her, and bent down to gather up the first aid box and the bowl of now bloody water he had used for Carlo.

Nina saw the blood and her head reeled. 'Is...is he going to be all right?' she breathed anxiously, dabbing at her tear-stained face with his handkerchief.

From the sink, Lorenzo turned to her and said, 'He'll be fine now—but, what is more to the point, are we going to be all right?'

Nina stared at him, not quite understanding but getting there gradually. The crisis with Carlo was over now and it was back to them. They were strongly attracted to each other and that couldn't be denied any more. In fact he had admitted it in the scented garden, the stone gods witness to it all. She knew how she felt and he must have guessed, but what was the answer? She licked her dry lips. 'I...I don't know,' she uttered helplessly.

He stood with his back to the sink, drying his hands and looking at her, a faint smile on his lips.

'You know, I learn more about you from how you are with Carlo than with me,' he told her.

Nina didn't understand that at all. It didn't have any relevance to where she thought this conversation was leading, not that she was very certain about that anyway.

'So...so what have you learned?' she asked daringly, though her voice was a mere whisper over the thudding of her heartbeat.

He didn't answer immediately, and she wondered what he was turning over in his mind.

And as she waited she nervously twisted the scrap of silk in her fingers.

'That you are sweet and caring and I'd rather like you to be the mother of my children,' he said softly.

Nina's blood didn't swoosh this time, it fairly raged through her arteries till she felt her head swim. Mother of his children? What sort of a remark was that?

She stood very still in the middle of the kitchen, the only sound the beat of her heart, which surely he must hear. Her throat was dry, her lips impossibly immobile, slightly apart with shock.

Slowly he came towards her, predatory but for a small smile at the edge of his well-defined lips. He lifted a hand and his thumb smoothed over her bottom lip, and then he gently closed her mouth for her with a slight tilt of her chin.

'Only one problem with that,' he murmured thickly. 'I'm not sure I can trust my own judgement any more. I see a sweet, caring, enigmatic young woman who talks to animals, and probably trees and grass for all I know. She is talented and has wit, and is strong at times and yet vulnerable at other times. And she confuses me greatly because above all else she has a sexuality she seems naively unaware of, and yet she is—or was—the mistress of a man whose demands are very high in that area.'

So they were back to Gio again, were they? Nina's heart sank.

His eyes locked with hers, dark and intense, searching for something she couldn't give him, something she suspected he wanted to hear. A denial of what he had just said, perhaps? For her to cry out that he had it all wrong and she wasn't and never had been the mistress of Gio Giulianni? Was that what he wanted from her?

By now he knew her well enough to know that she didn't fit the mould of a mistress, surely? But the evidence was weighted on his side. He had tracked her down because she had been making enquiries about Gio, and he knew him well enough to presume that they had had a relationship and that was the reason for her to be searching for him—the only reason in his thinking, because an illegitimate daughter from another country would never cross his mind.

And there was only one person in the world who could put him right, Nina thought unhappily. One sight of her and Gio would know she had never been his lover, but that one sight would never happen. It couldn't happen. At this moment in his life he wouldn't be able to bear the shock if the truth came out. He wouldn't want it and she didn't want to deliver it.

And suddenly she knew what this was all about, why Lorenzo said the things he did to her, why he looked at her so intently. That first kiss should have made things clear for her, his ardour and his passion which had remained in check until today when he had kissed her again and unwillingly admitted that he wanted her.

Though Nina had little experience of men, other than Jonathan and few light romances at art school, she wasn't naive enough to think Lorenzo hadn't deep passions flaming inside him. He was controlling himself, holding back from her, and she thought she knew the reason why now. Courageously she took a breath.

'Lorenzo, I think I know what you are trying to say.' She licked her dry lips and went on faintly. 'You are too proud to have an…an affair with me, because…because of Gio.'

Oh, God, was she really saying all this? She seemed to have grown up in leaps and bounds since meeting this man. She suddenly seemed to have a maturity she hadn't been aware of before.

'He…he is close to you,' she went on, 'and you are close to him, and you couldn't suffer the indignity of taking me…er…second hand.'

Her own words amazed her. She'd never thought she had it in her to be so outspoken about affairs. But she was sure she was right, certain, because of the way he was now looking at her. Nearly angry, almost astonished that she could say such a thing, but not indignant because she had got it wrong. No, she had got it right, and if he was angry it was because she had seen through him. But she wasn't put off by the dark frown that creased his brow now. She'd started and there was no way out of it but to go on.

She shrugged dismissively and spoke quietly and sensibly. 'I can't help you with your problem and your confusion and your pride—not wanting to lose face, Lorenzo. It's all down to you. You see, I'm not confused at all. There is nothing I can say or do that can make you feel any better about me. You either accept me as I am or not at all.'

She realised that that was almost an admission that she had been romantically involved with Gio in the past simply because she hadn't denied it and wasn't prepared to make any excuses for it. But it couldn't be any other way. It would be a lie to say that it was all over between her and Gio and to forget it because she cared for *him* now. A lie because it had never happened in the first place. But the truth was impossible too.

Lorenzo shook his dark head, struggling within. 'It isn't that easy,' he admitted roughly.

So she was on target, though she hadn't really needed further confirmation, but her heart was heavy at the thought that she wasn't in a position to help him in any way.

Slowly Nina lowered her head away from Lorenzo's searching gaze, unable to bear the weight of what she was suffering. The truth was always best, but impossible in this case. How *could* she tell him the truth? He *might* believe her that she was indeed Gio's daughter, but that would shift the weight of her dilemma to his shoulders. Knowing Gio for so long, being his greatest friend, he would feel obliged to tell all and...and it would prove to be a hornets' nest of emotions burst open almost on the eve of her father's wedding.

Nina shifted back from Lorenzo, out of temptation's way. She couldn't give either of them the freedom to take it any further. And perhaps that was for the best all round, and besides...another thought struck her. Wasn't she perhaps taking all this too deeply, too emotionally, too seriously? Lorenzo had admitted he wanted her, but he hadn't meant for life!

She looked down at herself, saw the state she was in; scruffy shorts, knees dusty where she had knelt in the dirt next to Carlo. It struck her how unsophisticated she was, so unlike Lorenzo who had the enviable talent of looking and being so sophisticated in whatever he chose to wear, even going barefoot in the heat did nothing to bring him down to a lesser level.

She *could* look sophisticated when she wanted to, with her hair up and her face made up, and she had nice clothes at home. But he had seen none of that, and if he did want her, did find her attractive, it was only because she was someone different in his life, someone transient.

And she knew that she wanted more, and the very thought was so unreal. She hadn't been ready for marriage to Jonathan because she hadn't truly loved him—but Lorenzo? Without even braving herself to look at him for confirmation of how she felt about him, she knew it was something far deeper than she had ever felt before.

She was going to be in some mess if this was love, and she rather suspected that this was it. She felt it in her heart, under her skin, in her very soul. His effect on her right from the very beginning had been a million times stronger than anything she had ever felt for any other man.

Mother of his children? The thought swayed her dizzily. The phrase evoked images of marriage and a family life full of warmth and love and caring, but to him it was simply a way of expressing himself, a sort of joke. He wanted her, yes, she believed that—physically—but it wasn't enough for a small-time girl like Nina Parker.

Shakily she crossed the kitchen back to Carlo, who

was sleeping on the blanket by the door. She knelt beside him, stroking him soothingly as he slept, her back to Lorenzo so he wouldn't see the anguish in her face.

Oh, God, what on earth was she doing here? She didn't belong. No one really wanted her the way she needed to be wanted. For what she was—simply Nina Parker.

A small whimper from Carlo brought her out of her self-pitying thoughts. She lifted her chin proudly and turned her face back to Lorenzo.

'Thank you for doing what you did for Carlo,' she told him, bright-eyed now. 'Do you mind him staying here in the kitchen till he's better? I promise he won't be any trouble and...'

Her voice trailed off. His eyes had narrowed and he looked angry again and she wondered what she had said now.

And then he swore—at least she guessed he was swearing—under his breath. Something not nice anyway, judging by the aggressive tone, but it was all in heated Italian that she didn't understand. His fists were clenched tightly at his sides and then he released them and seemed to have his temper under control again.

'Do what you think fit,' he said coldly. 'And don't bother with cooking for me tonight; I'm going out.'

Out? The very word seemed to slap her in the face. They had been living in an unreal world of isolation since she had arrived. Just the two of them in a secluded paradise where the world outside hadn't existed. Well, not for her anyway. But of course he had had the phone and his work, contact with business associates, Gio, probably, making wedding arrangements, and women, too, no doubt. It had never been like that for him.

Nina's shoulders sagged wearily and she lifted a limp hand to push her hair back from her face. A fool's paradise, that was what she had been living in with him. She gave herself a severe mental shakedown.

She got up from the floor. Bravely she smiled, as if his plans for the evening didn't concern her—because after all she was employed here, wasn't she?

'Suits me. I'll leave something cold for you just in case you are hungry when you get back.'

He didn't even thank her, just held her eyes momentarily in that old look of intensity which Nina could only interpret as puzzlement—though she could be very wrong in that assumption. More like contempt, when she really thought about it. Contempt for her being the mistress of his best friend and pyschologically blocking his way to seducing her!

Oh, I'm being paranoid, she thought after he had gone. Letting everything get on top of me and thinking too deeply about everything he says and the way he looks at me. He probably looked that way because I was naive enough to suggest a cold supper when he probably has no intentions of coming back till daybreak anyway!

The evening without him stretched interminably. If she hadn't had Carlo to look after she thought she might have gone silently mad—or noisily mad, even.

The house was gloomy and bleak without him, and only a short while back she had been thinking it was the most wondrous place to live and had never wanted to leave it.

Nightfall came and Nina switched on all the lights for comfort, but it didn't help. Outside it seemed hotter and closer than ever, and a deep rumble of thunder in the distance made her shiver. Just her luck to have to weather a storm alone with a sick dog in this huge spooky old house.

She made sure Carlo was comfortable in the kitchen, with fresh water and a bowl of food in case he woke hungry, then propped the kitchen door open. It was insufferably hot and Carlo might need to go outside in the night. If the rain came in she could mop it up in the morning, before Lorenzo saw it and went mad at her for being so careless.

She sensed that nothing would be the same again between them. He had his pride to consider, of course, because what she had done this day was effectively to reject him. And he couldn't handle the thought of her being Gio's mistress. He was jealous, couldn't put it out of his mind and forget it. So he *did* have feelings for her.

But she couldn't help him, and, besides, just how deep were those feelings?

The storm broke at midnight. Nina was still awake and she lay and listened to the wind lashing the rain against the shutters and the red terracotta tiles of the roof. Her ears ached with straining to hear Lorenzo returning but she heard nothing.

Half an hour later the bedside lamp flickered off and the bathroom light yielded nothing. It was so hot. The rain had done nothing to cool the air. Lighting a candle at the bedside, she realised why there were candles everywhere—the slightest hiccup in the weather and the power was cut.

In her short cotton nightie, she took matches and lit the candles in their sconces along the corridor and landing at the top of the stairs. When and *if* Lorenzo returned he would need to see his way to bed. She carried on down the stairs to check to see Carlo was all right in the kitchen.

She smiled as she stroked his head. He was sleeping contentedly, oblivious to the rain and the wind. He had eaten the food she had left for him so she knew he was well on the way to recovery.

Nina made her way back upstairs, slightly nervously

as the candles threw creepy shadows along the corridor. She was glad to get back into her bedroom and crawl under the sheet and bury her head in her pillow. She wished Lorenzo was back in the house because the wind was howling like crazy now and made her feel more tense than ever.

She was afraid, she realised. If the roof tore off, if a tree branch was ripped from its trunk and crashed through the window, if the wind caught a candle and set the old house on fire, if...

She awoke screaming, a weight crushing her chest. The stone statues were gathered around her bed, wet and naked and full of foreboding, laughing at her, jeering at her. *'Neenah, Neenah,'* they taunted.

'Nina, Nina, it's all right. I'm here. You're having a nightmare!'

Nina blinked open her eyes. She was damp with perspiration, her head spinning. The statues receded into the distance, the taunts faded, and there was just Lorenzo holding her, safely and securely in his arms. *On her bed and holding her tightly.*

Her mouth was chewing into his wet shirt-front. She couldn't speak. The horrors of the stormy night were still tight in her throat. Had she been screaming?

Oh, but she was safe now. Lorenzo was here and she was safe. She clung to him like a mad limpet, her heartbeat levelling and then pulsing up again as she felt the fierceness of his heartbeat outdoing her own.

She pulled back from him and stared at him. He was soaking wet, like the statues in her nightmare, but he wasn't taunting her. His eyes were soft and dark, showing concern and yet relief that she was all right. The rain had tightened the spirals of curls on his head and she had to hold back from reaching up and touching them in wonderment. Oh, how she had longed to do that since first meeting him, to run her fingers through that enviable hair.

At last her voice came in a hysterical burst. 'Oh, that was awful,' she gasped, her grey eyes wide and staring. 'The statues had come to get me and the wind was taunting me and—'

'And it's all right, darling, just a bad dream, and I should never have left you.' His grip on her tightened in comfort.

'I…I haven't had dreams like that since I was a child,' she blurted feverishly. 'When they told me…when I knew I didn't belong… They didn't understand…no one understood…and I was alone…all alone—'

'But you're not now, Nina, darling, not now. I'm here. I'm here with you.'

The deep resonance of his sincerity brought Nina fully awake. She shook her head slightly and lowered her chin. Oh, God, what had she said?

'I'm all right now,' she murmured, and tried to loosen herself from his grip but he held her firmly.

'You're not, and I'm going downstairs to get you some brandy. It will calm you down. Stay where you are,' he ordered tenderly.

She felt the weight of his body lift from the bed and she only just stopped herself from clutching at him to keep him with her. But she wasn't a child, she told herself sternly.

Bright-eyed, she watched him walk out of the room and then she closed her eyes in her suffering and pulled the sheet up around her neck. She felt so foolish, so, so silly for allowing a nightmare to claim his attention. He must have just got home, heard her crying out, cursed himself and wondered what madness had made him seek her out in the first place.

She was nothing but a liability to him, some half-crazed silly, frivolous female who was terrified of the dark and…and he had called her *darling*!

Had he? Now she wasn't sure. The remnants of the nightmare still hovered like shrouds of ghostly mist, clouding her senses. But if he *had* called her darling it had only been because she was some poor thing that he'd needed to use imagination to calm down.

By the time Lorenzo returned with a decanter of brandy and two glasses, and a towel looped around his neck to catch the drips of rainwater from his hair, Nina had her equilibrium on line again. Quickly she had dived into the bathroom to sponge her face and cast off her damp nightie and throw on a clean white T-shirt for propriety's sake. She was back in bed now, propped up against the downy pillows and ready to make her apologies.

'I'm sorry for giving you all this trouble. The lights went and the storm must have sent me a little mad. What with Carlo and everything, I suppose I was a bit stressed out.'

'And I didn't help,' Lorenzo admitted with a small smile as he handed her a goblet of golden liquid.

Nina took it and managed a small smile for him. 'It was nothing to do with you. You have every right to go out. It was just unfortunate you picked the night of a thousand storms.'

Perched on the edge of the bed, he looked at her intently. 'I didn't mean that. It didn't cross my mind that a courageous young woman who had hitchhiked alone through Europe would be at all worried by spending an evening alone in the house. And I think if all had been well between us before I left, you wouldn't have suffered a nasty nightmare,' he concluded softly.

Nina's protestation burst from her lips in a half-laugh. 'Gosh, you have some ego. *You* didn't cross my mind all evening.'

'And you're not a very good liar,' he said teasingly.

Nina gulped at the brandy and just managed to hold back a gauche choke as it hit the back of her throat. She swallowed hard, but all the same her voice came out in a fire-induced croak.

'Lorenzo, if you have a guilty conscience about leaving me alone, forget it.'

'I haven't a guilty conscience about leaving you alone, though I shouldn't have done. I only have a guilty conscience for treating you the way I have. You're right. I suffer with my dignity and pride and—' he shrugged helplessly '—and I'm having difficulty in understanding my own reasoning.'

Nina raised a brow. 'Perhaps you've been too long out of the courtroom.' She drew her knees up, wrapped her arms around them and let the goblet hang loosely in one hand. It was almost empty. 'Back in New York you'll buzz again,' she told him with a small grin. 'Here in your home country you are letting your brain go cold.'

He nodded and smiled. 'At this moment in time I never want to go back,' he told her softly, and his eyes held hers so deeply and meaningfully she had to look away.

Her pulses were rushing again. Did he mean that because of her? It was a delicious thought but highly improbable she thought sensibly. He belonged back in New York and she would soon be going back to England where she belonged—except she thought she belonged to Sicily now. It was in her heart, under her skin, in her soul. Just as he was.

She gulped the last of her brandy and put the glass down on the bedside table. She was sleepy now and wanted to curl up and let the golden pacifier drift her off to her dreams, the ones that never came true but helped pass the long night.

'What did you mean just now, about your childhood and being alone, no one understanding?'

Nina stared at him, her own incoherent mutterings coming back to her and washing over her with embarrassment.

'Oh, nothing, really. It…it doesn't matter.'

'But I'd like to know,' he persisted, refilling both their glasses and lifting hers till she had no choice but to take it from him. 'You've never spoken of your family.'

'Nor you,' she countered.

'You know that Gio has taken the place of a father I lost when I was but a child.' He smiled thinly. 'And you know my mother is a collector of stone effigies that have frightened the life out of you tonight.'

Nina laughed. 'Perhaps I don't want to meet her after all,' she joked.

'So what about your own parents? Have you any brothers and sisters?'

Nina fidgeted her feet slightly under cover of the sheet. She didn't really want to say anything about her past, but…but the brandy was softening her reserve and whatever she told Lorenzo, well, it didn't much matter because not in a million light years would he realise the true reason she was here in Sicily.

'No brothers and sisters,' she told him. 'I would have liked some—even one.' She smiled reflectively, staring at the satin binding of the sheet that was around her knees. 'My parents couldn't have children, you see. My mother is a teacher and my father a lecturer and, well, really they should never have had me because they are professional people and I never really fitted in with them. But I suppose at one time in their lives—' she shrugged '—well, I suppose they thought they had it all except a child, and they just got me as if they were adding to their collection of material objects. They told me when I was old enough to understand and somehow it all fitted.

They aren't very warm people, and, well, perhaps it might have been different if I really had been theirs, but—'

'Nina,' Lorenzo interrupted.

Her head shot up and she looked at him, wondering what she had said for him to interrupt so harshly.

'Are you, were you…were you adopted?'

His voice was thick and gravelly, a bit like her head at the moment. Oh, she had said too much. Now he might feel sorry for her, and already tonight she had made an absolute fool of herself by having a childish nightmare.

She jutted her chin. 'Yes, I was,' she admitted truthfully, and then she smiled and wasn't quite so truthful. 'They are ever so successful, you know. They are in Australia at the moment, both on some exchange scheme for a year. I'll probably join them after Si…Sicily.' She yawned suddenly. 'I'm halfway there, after all. Yes, I might join them. They've written and asked me to go down, and…and they are missing m-me…'

Oh, God, the brandy was filling her eyes with tears. With all her might she willed them back, and managed to grin sheepishly at Lorenzo, who was watching her with such deep intensity.

'I…I need to sleep now,' she murmured drowsily, and slid down the bed and leaned her heavy head back against the pillows. 'You will make sure Carlo is all right before you go to bed, won't you? He seems fine, but…'

Her head swam and her eyes burned and she felt Lorenzo shift the cool sheet up under her chin, and then she remembered no more.

But when she awoke as bright sunlight filtered through the shutters she remembered everything. With a soft groan of dismay she turned her head to one side and her nostrils were filled with a delicious lemony scent that had her blood rushing hotly.

Lorenzo was asleep beside her on the bed.

CHAPTER SEVEN

FOR a few minutes Nina lay very still. Lorenzo had stayed with her through the night. She remembered the storm, the nightmare and waking to find him standing over her. And more—the brandy, and talking softly to him about her parents.

He knew she was adopted now but he couldn't know any more. It would take a miracle man to get anything constructive out of her feeble confessions brought on by a glass of fiery brandy that had loosened her tongue.

So that was probably the reason he had stayed with her through the night. To keep an eye on an inebriated Nina Parker who might have got up, floundered her way to the top of the landing and fallen headfirst down the stairs!

She smiled softly to herself. Or maybe he was here simply because he couldn't bear to be apart from her any longer. She sighed wistfully. Whatever the reason, the feeling was good. Him lying soundly asleep next to her, wanting to protect her and keep her safe.

She shifted slightly. The sheet lay between their warm bodies. The sheet and her T-shirt and his... She dared take a peek. He lay on his back on the top of the sheet and was wearing the bottoms of a pair of dark navy silk pyjamas. He was naked from the waist up, excitingly naked and bronzed, with black tight curls down his chest, and he looked just wonderful.

Nina cautiously moved again, very, very carefully up onto one elbow, her hand supporting her head and her silken flax-coloured hair a shimmering curtain down her arm.

She knew then, without a doubt, that she loved Lorenzo Biacci, and this morning, when all was calm and peaceful with the world, the feeling was delicious. Perhaps this would be the only time she could readily give in to the luxury of loving him so deeply. Because he was asleep and not watching her so intently and making her feel wary inside.

His hair was dry now, the spirals of curls loosened slightly to hang around his handsome face. He was more beautiful than any sculpture his mother had collected. The mythological gods would have been proud to have him as one of their own.

Tentatively she reached out and with the tips of her fingers took hold of one of those spirals of hair and was astonished at the soft silkiness of it. She wanted to spread all of her fingers in the coiled mass and lower her head and feel his hair on her face and her lips.

And why not? He was very deeply asleep. She closed her eyes and leaned forward and it was everything she'd expected it to be. Warm, silky, scented. Sensuously she pursed her lips and pressed the springy coils to her mouth, gently rubbed her full lips across them. If she never got any closer to him this would be enough. To adore him so without him knowing.

He murmured slightly but didn't awaken, and Nina went on enjoying her adoration of him. She moved the open palm of her hand over his chest, not touching but revelling in the heat from his body. And then she could hold back no longer and slowly lowered her palm till she was touching him—small, tentative caresses.

And she wanted her mouth to enjoy the sensation too, and as he was breathing so deeply and regularly she did what her heart was crying out to do. She lowered her warm lips to his chest and let them savour the taste of him, the scent of him, the *mystique* of him.

Her arousal, making her dizzy with sensation, her

limbs liquid and heavy, urged her to take more. She let the tip of her tongue lightly lap over the coils of springy hair on his chest. He let out a soft moan but still he didn't awaken.

Nina drew back from him and smiled wickedly. It was like taking forbidden fruit, all the more daring and exciting because it hadn't been offered. But she wanted the whole orchard, she realised. She ached to possess it all. His mouth, his body, his heart, the very core of him.

What had happened to her since coming to Sicily? He had seen it, the sensuality she hadn't known she had. The sun, the heat, the beauty of this magical island had brought it all out. Maybe it was because she had found her homeland—except that...

No, she couldn't think of anything else but this moment. Nothing else existed. Just him and the morning sunlight filtering through the shutters. *He* made her feel this way.

And she took. Unable to resist it, she leaned over his mouth, closed her eyes to enhance the feeling, and pressed her lips over his. Her blood sang, her heart hummed, she was so vibrantly alive her whole body tingled with sensation. She was up there, in some place she had never been before, soaring like a bird, free and alone...

Except she wasn't alone. Lorenzo was flying with her, his mouth moving under hers, lifting her higher and higher.

And then she was falling, and the sudden loss of gravity brought her eyes open wide. Suddenly Lorenzo was over her instead of her over him, and he was smiling, and his eyes were heavy and slumberous and not one bit angry with her for taking such liberties.

'I knew that pink flush went further than your face,' he murmured softly. He ran the back of his hand over her throat, down further still, beyond the loose cotton of her T-shirt. And then he was lifting it all from her back.

'You see?' he breathed deeply as he looked down on her naked form. 'And just as I painted you, wanton and wanting.'

His mouth closed over hers and Nina didn't protest. How could she? Wasn't he everything she wanted in life? And hadn't she been so daring with her exploration knowing that he couldn't fail to respond to it? Her way of making it easy for him because words couldn't do it? Yes, she supposed she was a tricky lady, as he had said, but he had made her that way.

She languished in the kiss, let it all flow out of her. She was unashamed of what she had done—touched him so intimately, pressed his hair to her mouth, kissed him before he kissed her. It was right, so what matter who made the moves?

He was holding her so tightly, arms wrapped around her as if never to let her go. His mouth, so warm and sensuous, trailed over her skin, setting it on fire till she could hardly breathe with excitement.

'Lorenzo,' she murmured.

The tips of his fingers stilled her lips. 'No, *bellisima*, no questions, no answers. Nothing to be said to talk your way out of this,' he said softly. 'It was destined and you can't change destiny. Be still now, let me love you as I've wanted to do since first sight of you.'

Nina clung to him, squeezing her eyes tight with happiness. *Que sera, sera,* she thought mistily, and lost herself to his passion and ardour.

And it was so easy to take pleasure in everything he did to her. And so easy for her to pleasure him till his breath quickened heatedly. She had so little experience, but suddenly she knew it all and wanted to do everything with him. She touched and spread her fingers around him through the dark blue silk, and then hungrily clawed at his pyjamas to release him. And then she was melded against his naked skin and burning and burning with need.

But Lorenzo was a sensual lover. He paced it all as if it were choreographed. Each movement calculated to give the most intense pleasure. Each intimate exploration of her body so deep and meaningful it swelled her love for him like some hothouse flower gently coaxed into early blooming and displaying its beauty for the world to envy.

And as the heat inside her rose it suddenly changed. They were fire together, raging, and breathing so fast it was impossible to control. The urgency couldn't be abated or even slowed. Her breasts were swollen beneath his hands and his mouth, full and aching for him, the sensitivity of her nipples sending alarming signals down between her thighs.

She moaned helplessly when he held her hips with the spread of his strong hands and lowered his mouth to the most secret part of her. Her body arched up against him as if in human sacrifice; she wanted to die in that moment of ecstasy as he drew deeply on her, tasting her, lapping at her till she was crying for a release she knew little about but sensed she was on the brink of discovering for the first time.

But Lorenzo teased, held her back, controlled her passion till she gasped wildly to be released.

'Together,' he breathed heavily, and moved across her, parted her thighs and pressed himself urgently into her.

Nina bit hard on her tongue, desperate to hold back the cry of pain she was anticipating, but it never came and the moment of panic was over, and then all was heat and fire as she closed herself around him as he moved inside her.

And it was wondrous, spinning her senses till nothing

but his urgency and her need mattered in the whole wide world. Long, smooth strokes of pure pleasure and then a swamping feeling of unreality as the pumping grew more intense.

Her body burned, her head reeled, and she was crying and clawing him, and he was wet and powerful, his magnificent body thudding against hers, driving her harder and harder till she cried out, a long, anguished moan of release, which he matched with his own anguished roar of release which collapsed him over her burning body, his mouth and face buried in her damp hair.

She held him tightly to her for what seemed like for ever, raked her fingers through the tight coils of his hair, free to do it now, free to do whatever she liked to him because they were as one.

He was the first to speak—something in Italian, low murmurings.

'I don't understand,' she moaned softly in his ear, wishing she had studied languages.

He lifted his dark head and looked down on her. His smile was warm and relaxed. 'You will one day,' he whispered, 'when you learn my language.'

Nina melted inside. That sounded as if they would be together for ever.

A sudden howl at the bedroom door and an alarming scrabbling sound put paid to Nina pressing for just a little more of this togetherness thing that filled her heart with happiness.

Lorenzo laughed softly and bent his head to playfully rub her nose with his. 'My worst nightmare coming true,' he ground out as he swung his legs from the bed.

Nina lay back in the bed, laughing as, naked, he padded across the room to open the door. She knew exactly who was on the other side of it.

Carlo hurtled through the door, almost before it was fully open. His claws clicked on the polished wooden floor, he skidded, skilfully corrected himself, in doing so shooting a heavy rug across the room, and in one bound leapt onto the bed, his weight nearly bouncing Nina off.

'For heaven's sake, Carlo,' she shrieked as he lunged at her, nuzzling her face till she had to grab hold of his ears to keep him from ravishing her. 'This isn't the time or the place!'

'I wholeheartedly echo that,' Lorenzo grumbled as he came back to the bedside.

He spoke heatedly and decisively in Italian to Carlo, who swiftly gave him short shrift in his own reply: a deep rumble of a growl and bared teeth to go with it.

'You ungrateful swine!' Lorenzo bellowed at him in English.

Nina couldn't stop laughing as she clung to Carlo's neck, just in case he thought of charging Lorenzo.

'He's a dog not a pig,' she laughed at Lorenzo. Then she gave her attention to the dog, turned his face to her so he wouldn't miss a word she said. 'He's right, Carlo. You have a very short memory. Lorenzo probably saved your life yesterday. Now, you ungrateful mutt, think on that—because if you fall out with Lorenzo you fall out with me. Got it?'

Carlo gave a small whimper of submission and settled down on the bed next to her, giving Lorenzo a very cautious look with his big brown eyes.

Lorenzo shrugged helplessly and snatched at his pyjama bottoms from the foot of the bed. He grumbled constantly in Italian as he hauled them on, which had Nina giggling even more.

'I dare you to come back to bed,' she teased.

Lorenzo smiled thinly. 'Not on your life. Once bitten twice shy.' He came and leaned over her, hands each side of her for support. He nuzzled her neck and kissed her warmly on her expectant lips and then murmured,

'And don't take that personally. I was referring to him not you. Where you are concerned once will never be enough.'

Glowing with happiness, Nina linked her arms around his neck and kissed him fully on the mouth, a long, long kiss full of all her love, and when she drew back she grinned at him.

'You see? Carlo loves you now. He would never have let me do that to you a few days ago.'

Lorenzo, still leaning over her, signalled with his eyes and Nina looked to where he was indicating.

She burst out laughing again as she saw that all the time Lorenzo had been leaning over her he had one powerful hand firmly clutching at Carlo's throat, to restrain him, just in case!

With a wide grin he moved then, and in rapid Italian gave Carlo an order which, unbelievably, he obeyed. He leapt off the bed and padded across the room and immediately sat by the door and waited.

'What on earth did you say to him?' Nina asked, her eyes wide with disbelief.

Lorenzo stood by the door grinning back at her. 'I told him that if he ever attempted to come into this room again he would be preventing you from becoming the mother of my children. I think he's got the message. One or two eggs for breakfast?' he added.

Nina happily slid down the bed under the very crumpled sheet. 'Ten, I think. I'm starving.'

'Ten it will be, then,' he muttered as he closed the door behind him and Carlo.

Nina blissfully closed her eyes. And she had got the message too. Mother of his children? It could only mean one thing, Lorenzo's feelings were the same as her own. He loved her and wanted her in his life and she was so, so happy.

Wherever he had gone last night, he had gone to mull

over what she had accused him off, his crippling pride and what it was doing to him. And he had come back to her with it all controlled in his mind and wanting her, unconditionally.

But suddenly she bit her lip worriedly as she slid out of the bed and slipped on her T-shirt to go to the bathroom. He must know for sure now that she had never been Gio's mistress because although she had let herself go with their lovemaking she had been a novice after all.

A virgin, actually, she mused as she ran the shower. And he must have known. But then perhaps not, because in the heat of passion it might not have occurred to him. It had all come so naturally to her anyway. She had lost all inhibitions with him because that was the way he had made her feel. Free and sensual, their lovemaking coming as naturally as morning rain in an English April.

Nina stood with her back to the cool tiles and let the warm water tingle her skin fully awake, and with her new clear thinking came a sudden loss of euphoria.

Her conscience troubled her deeply. She was burdened with this secret she held in her heart, the secret of her identity. Now that they were lovers they would grow closer, and undoubtedly Gio would be discussed again, and Lorenzo would ask, If you never were Gio's mistress why were you searching for him?

Hands shaking, Nina reached for the shower handle and shut off the water. She stood frozen to the spot, letting the silence heap on her, bringing her down and down till all her happiness drained out of her.

It was all impossible, she thought in panic. How could she be a part of Lorenzo's life when…? Panic had really got a hold now. She was shaking with it. She nearly slipped getting out of the shower and clutched at the side of the glass door for support.

She sat tensely on the edge of the bed, punishingly

drying her legs with a towel. If Lorenzo did want to
marry her, then…then what? *Then* she would be a part
of his life, and Lorenzo was a part of her father's life
and…and she might be invited to her father's wedding.
Oh, dear God, she *would* be invited. She would meet her
father at last, her half-sister and this Sofia he was going
to marry—the one woman he should have married a long
time ago but for some dreadful circumstance that had
kept them apart till now.

She shivered, shook to the very soles of her bare feet.
Could she keep this heart-wrenchingly painful secret to
herself? Could she meet her father and hold back her
identity? Hadn't she burned to be reunited with him?
For years hadn't she dreamt of knowing him and being
drawn into his life, as it should have been from the very
day she had been born?

She felt so horribly cheated suddenly. To be so close
and to have it all snatched out of her reach because of
her love for Lorenzo.

'You bloody fool!' she breathed as a wave of sensibil-
ity washed over her.

She should have told Lorenzo from the very start, but
she hadn't known she was going to fall in love with him.
Now her love was a complication that was driving her
ever deeper into subterfuge. And what an idiot she was
being now, in thinking she could get away with it.

'I've got to tell him now!' she breathed to herself.
'The truth, the whole truth and nothing but the truth.'

She got up and pulled some clothes from her wardrobe, a thin shirt and the old cinnamon-coloured skirt
again. Oh, hell, she wished she had some decent clothes.
Oh, hell, why had she put herself through so much tor-
ment when the truth from the off would have been for
the best?

Perhaps she could swear Lorenzo to secrecy, not to
reveal her identity to her father. Maybe later it could all

come out, after the wedding, when perhaps tensions wouldn't be so high. Maybe Lorenzo might think it prudent not to mention it *ever*!

And for the moment she couldn't bear to think of that. It was too much to cope with. This was enough, more than enough, having to admit to Lorenzo just why she had been looking for Gio Giulianni.

Nina glared at her simple travelling clothes. Because she had been hitchhiking she hadn't brought anything remotely pretty. She stared at the motley collection of lightweight easy-to-roll clothes. She so badly wanted to look different this morning. To look pretty for Lorenzo.

Tentatively she pulled the blue dress he had given her to wear from the back of the wardrobe. She couldn't wear it, of course. It belonged to…she didn't know who it belonged to because she had never pressed to know. Blindly she had pushed the thought that he had a lover to the back of her mind because she just didn't want to know!

She gazed at the dress enviously. It was the sort of dress she would like to wear, but her envy wasn't just because it was so nice and wasn't hers. Whoever it belonged to had been or perhaps still was a part of Lorenzo's life.

'And you should have found out more before you so…so naively gave your heart to him,' she whispered to herself.

She slammed shut the wardrobe door fiercely. This was ridiculous! *She* was a part of his life now, not the owner of that dress.

She pulled on her own clothes, combed her hair till it was tamed and shining. She was determined not to let anything spoil her happiness this morning. She grinned at her reflection. 'Think positively,' she mouthed. 'After this wondrous morning with Lorenzo you have nothing to fear, you idiot!' And when she braved herself to tell him the truth of who she was he would understand because he cared about her.

She went straight downstairs, just as the phone was ringing in the spacious stone-floored hallway. The huge double oak doors were open to let in the sunlight and she smiled, remembering her first steps into this hall, expecting an army of servants and family to be waiting. Thank heavens they hadn't been! She'd had Lorenzo all to herself.

She was on the bottom step when Lorenzo strode towards the phone, snatching it up and seeing her for the first time.

'I've left bacon grilling. Save it, darling, before it burns.'

Nina grinned and went towards the passageway that led to the kitchen, and then she stopped dead, out of Lorenzo's sight but close enough to hear the anxiety in his tone as he spoke into the phone.

'No, Gio, definitely not!' he snapped in English, and then switched to rapid Italian.

Nina was transfixed for a moment, curious to know what was being said but not understanding a word of it, only knowing by his tone that Lorenzo seemed angry.

And he was speaking to her father and it made her feel so strange inside. She supposed Lorenzo had spoken to him often while she had been staying here but...but now it was all different.

She rescued the bacon, turned down the grill, quickly assessed how far breakfast had gone and what she could do. She went to the fridge for eggs and stopped. The noticeboard was by the side of the fridge, and though she had looked at that photo a thousand times it seemed different this morning.

And she knew why immediately, and her head spun. Of course. She gulped and studied it more intently, hoping perhaps she was wrong—but she wasn't. It was because she had only just looked at the silky blue dress this morning and it was fresh in her mind.

Her half-sister was wearing it in the photograph as she was clinging possessively to Lorenzo's arm.

By the time Lorenzo came back into the kitchen she had convinced herself that it didn't matter. In fact it was better than it belonging to anyone else. This was Lorenzo's home, and of course Gio, and his daughter, would have been here many times, probably stayed over, even spent weekends here. And, though it was possible that Lorenzo and her half-sister were close, that didn't mean that they had had an affair...or were still having one!

Her hands were shaking so much that suddenly the eggs had dropped out of her fingers and smashed on the tiles. She stared at them and then swung round to apologise to Lorenzo, a nervous laugh on the edge of her lips, ready to make a joke of it to cover her sudden apprehension.

But he hadn't even noticed.

Nina's insides tightened. He was standing in the kitchen doorway, shoulders tensed under a white silk shirt, looking out over the terrace and the gardens. He didn't speak. Just stood rigid against the doorway as if she wasn't there, as if she didn't exist for him any more.

Nina silently cleared up the mess she had made, so nervous now she couldn't speak herself. Something had changed since Lorenzo had taken that phone call. He was different. And she was different, too. She was doubting his love suddenly. Her head swam with it all. Lorenzo's sudden detachment from her, that wretched dress, her father, her half-sister....

'Bring the coffee out onto the terrace, Nina,' Lorenzo suddenly commanded, so shortly that Nina jerked with shock.

She watched him step out onto the terrace without

even turning to look at her. She felt as if she had been slapped back into place—the hired help, not the woman he had made love to earlier.

Lorenzo strode over to the top of the terrace steps and just stood there, still tense, still so distracted from her, shoulders hunched, arms wrapped around himself, gazing out over the gardens. She wished she could see his face because then she might see what the problem was. But that was crazy. She had never been able to guess his moods, and just because they were lovers now it was naive to think she knew him any better.

She took the tray of coffee out to him and set it on the terrace table, which was still wet from the night's deluge. She was about to go back into the kitchen to get a cloth when he spoke.

'I have something to tell you,' he said gravely. 'I should have told you from the very beginning but it didn't need to be said then. Now it does, of course, because things have changed between us.'

Still he couldn't bring himself to face her, and because of that Nina's heart sank. If it wasn't something serious he would face her with it. So it was time for baring the soul, putting her down and out of his life because their lovemaking this morning hadn't meant anything to him and he wanted to make some sort of an excuse for letting his passion run away with him. And suddenly she knew what the something was he wanted to tell her. Talking with Gio had reminded him.

'It…it's all right,' she told him quickly, defensively. She used two hands to pour the coffee for extra support. She felt so suddenly weak that if a puff of wind galloped up the terrace steps it would bowl her over. 'I half expected it, really,' she went on, drawing up her strength from somewhere deep inside her. 'I'm as equally to blame for letting it happen. Well, starting it all, really, by kissing you when you weren't even awake.'

She gulped more air. 'I mean it was pushy of me, and I'm sorry because it has complicated everything. You're right. I am naive. I just wanted it to happen without thinking of the consequences. I should have asked you about...' She gave a short, nervous laugh. 'I don't even know her name. My...your...Gio's daughter—your lover. I mean I should have known. The photo says it all. She obviously adores you, and I did have my suspicions but I didn't really want to know. I pushed it out of my mind. So it isn't your fault and, well...well...I want you to know that you don't have to feel bad about what happened between us.'

Carefully she put the coffee pot down on the table before it went the same way as the eggs. She lifted her head. She had his full attention now. He was glaring at her, it was the glare to end all glares, and her heart nearly stopped. But her mouth couldn't stop because she had to salvage some pride out of all this. She gabbled on, even laughed. She did everything in her power to cover her own anguish and make light of it all.

'These things happen.' She managed a dismissive shrug of her shoulders. 'Men and women do it all the time, you know—make...have sex. It was nice but...but—'

'Nice!'

His sudden explosion of anger made her jump. She clenched her fists at her sides to steady herself. With two strides he was upon her and grasping her shoulders so harshly she winced. His eyes were blacker than she had ever seen them before. His mouth was working but Nina could hardly grasp at what he was saying she was so frightened.

'Are you trying to tell me that our lovemaking was nothing more than *nice*?' he bellowed.

And then Nina was angry too. Here he was, about to

confess all about his lover, and he was suddenly angry with her for trying to make it easier for him.

'You're hurting me,' she cried. 'And how dare you get all mad with me? If it's your damned insufferable Sicilian pride resurfacing then you should have thought of it an hour or so ago. But I suppose that was too much to ask when faced with my willing compliance,' she scathed contemptuously. 'It was that phone call this morning that changed everything, wasn't it? Suddenly you were hauled back into the land of the living. Gio rang and it reminded you of what you really think of me and, oh, let's not forget what you are trying to tell me now, your commitment to his daughter and—'

And suddenly he had folded her into his arms, and she was crying and biting into his shirt again and he was soothing her.

'Oh, Nina, Nina,' he groaned into her hair. 'Cristina is close to me, yes. Is this what all this is about? You're jealous?'

She pushed at him then, blinked away those treacherous tears and gazed up into his drawn face.

'And…and don't try and dismiss it with soft words, Lorenzo,' she bit out, eyes blazing now. How typical of a man to try and make the woman the guilty one! 'And jealousy isn't what I'm feeling at all. It's more disappointment in myself for blindly dismissing your relationship with Cris—Cristina because I wanted you for myself. And anyway, you started all this, saying you had something to tell me. You're right—you should have told me sooner because it just isn't fair to me, or even fair to…to Cristina.'

'I wasn't about to tell you about Cristina—'

'Oh, you just thought she didn't matter any more! Don't say another word, Lorenzo, because you are beginning to dig your own grave and you'll be jumping into it next. Oh, what a fool I've been—'

'Yes, a fool, Nina, an adorable, silly little fool, and it's why I love you so.'

And now he was mocking her, treating her as if she were a child. Nina leapt back out of his reach, not wanting him to hug her to him and try to make more excuses.

But he...he'd said he loved her... Did he? Hopefully she searched his face for the truth, and though his mouth was smiling there was still a degree of anxiety in his eyes which cast a shadow of doubt on what he had just said. Was it just lip service? Or had she simply misheard?

'Cristina,' she breathed quickly, hardly able to think coherently, 'you *weren't* going to tell me about her?'

His shoulders sagged and Nina's went up defensively, preparing herself for the truth now that she had forced him into a confession. Yes, they had been lovers once, now it was all over, because of her, and now he was going to tell Cristina and... Oh, God, now she felt so terribly guilty.

'No, it isn't what I was about to tell you, but now you've brought it up I will. Cristina is not my lover and never has been, Nina,' he told her solemnly, making no attempt to reach out to her this time. 'She's my sister; that's why.'

Nina reeled back even further from him, her whole body swaying with shock. *His sister?* Her face paled instantly as the blood drained from it. She thought she might pass out at his feet. Cristina was Gio's daughter, her half-sister, Lorenzo's *sister*! The permutations rocked Nina to her very soul.

She felt the chair at the back of her knees. Lorenzo was sitting her down in it. Lorenzo was smiling indulgently, sugaring her coffee for her, speaking, but Nina was hardly hearing what he was saying. All that raged through her head was that...

'We don't share the same father, though. She's my half-sister—'

'What?' Nina shrieked. Her eyes widened as the words sank in. Had she heard right? Had she been safely delivered from the jaws of hell? Of course—the realisation of a former conversation flooded her—he had said he loved Gio as a father because he didn't have one of his own. Gio wasn't *his* father.

Nina felt the blood wash through her veins again, cleansing her, purifying her. In a daze she lifted a hand to touch her brow, checking to see if she still had feeling and she wasn't in a dream. She moistened her dry lips before speaking. 'I'm sorry for shouting at you,' she said softly but she couldn't meet his eye because of her shame at what she had imagined she had done—made love to her half-brother.

It was all too much for her. She lifted the hot coffee to her lips and blinked out over the gardens. What a devil of a place this Sicily was. It turned your mind and sent you half-crazy.

'I...I'm sorry for thinking Cristina was your...' She shivered slightly and sipped more coffee, holding the cup with two hands to keep it steady. 'It never crossed my mind that she was your sister,' she added weakly. Not in a thousand years would it have done, either.

Cristina. She knew her name now and she should feel closer to her, but she felt ever more distanced. She might be her half-sister but she was also Lorenzo's half-sister. It was all getting worse instead of better.

She fully realised now that the phone call had been the key to his change of mood. When he had answered it he had been fine, had called her darling and asked her to save the bacon. And afterwards he had grown tense and she had thought it was because he had been reminded of his commitment to Cristina. So what had he

been about to tell her before she had gone to hell and
back on the wings of a mad bat?

She watched him warily over the rim of her coffee
cup as he sat across from her. He pulled his hair back
from his face, the coils of hair she had so lovingly
mouthed kisses over this very morning. And then it had
all gone wrong.

'Lorenzo,' she began, 'you wanted to tell me something.'

He held her eyes and smiled. 'Yes, but then you forestalled me with your accusations, but amongst all the
dross of it I heard a few things that made me understand
your insecurity.'

'Oh, yes?' she murmured, hardly able to recall just
what she had said now.

'Your feelings are the same as mine.'

Her heart began to thud.

'But you can't quite believe it has happened,' he
added, smiling at her.

Nina managed to bring a small smile to her own lips.
Very true. Insecurity, guilt over keeping the secret of her
identity so long from him, lack of confidence in herself—all had balled together, making her jump to all
manner of silly conclusions. He had loved her so passionately this morning and she should have known how
he truly felt.

'So...so what did you have to tell me?' she whispered.

'This is going to be difficult for me,' he stated. 'So
bear with me and hear me out. I should have told you
from the very start, but as I said I didn't know everything
was going to work out this way. Falling in love with
you.'

Nina lifted her chin and gazed at him, her grey eyes
moist and limpid, her heart brimming with happiness. It
was going to be all right and she was eager to tell it all

now because he loved her and he would help her through the emotional time ahead of her.

'And you do feel the same way, don't you, Nina?'

His sudden insecurity touched her deeply. To even ask such a thing when he must know. She laughed very softly.

'You're ever a surprise to me, Lorenzo. Yes, I feel the same way.' She leaned across the table to him, her eyes sparkling. 'Now will you please tell me what you were going to tell? Because until you do I can't feel free to wrap my arms around you and convince you properly.'

He reached out and took her hand and lifted it to his lips. His mouth was warm and full of love, and Nina felt freer than she had for a long time. She was soaring with happiness and she would tell him so in a minute, tell him how much she loved him and, yes, tell him just who she was.

He let her hand go. 'I'm sorry if I've appeared distracted and tense since Gio called. He omitted to tell me last night that—'

'Last night? You were with Gio last night?' she interjected quickly. She was surprised to hear that was where he had been.

Lorenzo directed his attention to the coffee pot, refilled their cups. Nina clenched her hands in her lap, waiting for his reply, her suspicions aroused because Lorenzo wasn't meeting her eyes.

'We had some wedding arrangements to go over,' he told her.

'You haven't seen him since I've been here. Wouldn't a phone call have sufficed?'

His eyes came back to hers then, and Nina further steeled herself. Why last night, after their row?

There was a long silence as he looked at her directly and intently.

'I had to know,' he said eventually.

'Know what?' Nina laughed nervously. Why was everything getting dark and gloomy again? Why was she feeling nervous so suddenly?

'I had to know whether or not you had ever been Gio's lover.'

Nina's insides folded. Her fists balled dangerously, cutting off the blood supply to her wrists. He had done that? Checked up on her...before...before returning to make love to her? She had thought he had that punishing pride under control. She had thought his love had come unconditionally.

'You have never denied it,' he went on levelly. 'And—'

'And you were curious,' she interrupted bitterly. Her lips twisted with contempt as she levered herself up from the chair. This hurt—badly. She gazed at him dully, still not quite believing that he could have done such a thing. 'And Gio told you, did he? Told you he had never heard of Nina Parker?'

'He didn't recognise you, either.' Lorenzo stood up and came around the table and tried to take hold of her hand, but she whipped it out of reach.

'Didn't recognise me!' she exclaimed, stepping back from him, not understanding but with all manner of thoughts winging through her head. Had Gio been here without her knowing? Actually seen her?

'Darling, listen. This isn't what I had to tell you. You are making it ever more difficult for me.'

'Just a minute! Hold on!' She held her palms up to still him, verbally and physically. 'He hasn't been here. I would have known, heard a car on the drive. You have no photograph of me...only—' Her voice cracked to a stop and then it surged forward brutally. 'The picture! The drawing you did of me! You bastard! You only did it so you could take it to Gio, to show him, to find out for sure if we had had an affair or not!' She was shaking with rage now, humiliated beyond belief. Lorenzo had shown that erotic picture of her to her father? She couldn't bear the thought of it.

'And if Gio had confirmed your worst fears and said he had bedded me, you wouldn't have done last night. Is that what you are telling me? You couldn't take me on face value. Oh, no, that miserable Sicilian pride of yours wouldn't allow for that. You arrogant swine,' she raged.

He caught her before she reached the top of the terrace steps. Held her firmly. His eyes were black with rage now.

'You never denied it,' he repeated fiercely. 'I had to know.'

'I shouldn't have needed to deny it! It should have been enough that you trusted me to know that whatever had been between Gio and me, it was over!'

'But there never had been anything between you so why didn't you deny it?' he accused darkly. 'What are you up to, Nina? What and why?'

Her whole body sagged in his grip and she lowered her eyes fearfully. She had been prepared to tell him everything but now she couldn't—or could she? She lifted her eyes to meet his glare, her mind searching for any reason that might make her understand what had driven him to do such a thing.

She could swallow her own pride and acknowledge his and come to terms with it. It must be hellish to live with a pride as tight and as unyielding as his. But it was his heritage, something born into him, and in time she might be able to accept it. If she didn't...there was no hope for them.

She ran the tip of her tongue over her lower lip, wavering. 'At first everything was so weighted against me,' she admitted in a small voice. 'You picked me up

out of the gutter and to you it must have looked awful.
I bore all your accusations, though it was painful to do
it, and then I hoped that when you got to know me it
wouldn't matter, that you would see that I wasn't all bad.
But why, Lorenzo? Why the need to seek confirmation
from Gio?' she asked plaintively.

His anger hadn't abated one bit. His grip on her tightened fearfully.

'Because it isn't just you and me,' he insisted passionately. 'This wedding of Gio's is so important.
Important to Cristina and Gio and myself, and more important to Sofia. And it's different now because of my
feelings for you. I want you in my life and I had to be
sure!'

And still she didn't understand. He read it in her uncertain eyes. His grip softened a little.

'When I picked you up in Palermo I had to keep you
out of harm's way because of the wedding. I fell in love
with you, a complication I hadn't foreseen. Now I know
that you were never involved with Gio in the first place,
but why you hid that from me I don't know. Later perhaps you will tell me, but for now there isn't time.'

Nina drew in her breath. What on earth was he trying
to say?

'Sofia and Cristina are on their way here from the
airport. They have been shopping in Milan. Gio didn't
tell me last night after we talked about you. He seemed
distracted suddenly, not his usual self. He rang this
morning to say he can't pick them up himself and they
are coming here direct. I wasn't prepared for that because I hadn't told you.'

'Told me what?' Nina cried helplessly.

His eyes narrowed sternly as he took a ragged breath.
'Sofia is Cristina's mother, and she is my mother, too,
Nina. Gio is marrying my mother.'

CHAPTER EIGHT

NINA lifted her chin and met Lorenzo's penetrating look. She was ice inside, the shock to her system acting as fast freeze on every sense she possessed. Her mind hurtled, though. It careered off into the wild blue yonder and settled on impossibility.

How could she ever admit the bond between her and Gio now? Lorenzo was so deeply involved in Gio's wedding, more strongly and more deeply than she could have imagined. Sofia was Lorenzo's mother, Cristina's too, and Gio was Cristina's father but not Lorenzo's, and Gio was marrying the mother of his daughter, which made Cristina, at the moment, illegitimate, too. What a mess!

Nina wasn't even prepared to ask how this tangled web of relationships had ever evolved because one thing stood out above all else. She wasn't one of them.

She was Nina Parker, the English illegitimate daughter of Gio Giulianni who sounded as if his life was complicated enough without her crawling out from under a stone to reveal herself. The sooner she got away from here the better. If she stayed the truth would come out, because Lorenzo would still want to know why she had come to Sicily, and the truth was impossible.

'If…if your mother is coming home I'd better get the house cleaned up before I leave, then,' she told him levelly. Oh, she had it all well under control now.

Lorenzo's hands dropped to his sides. He looked startled, his eyes dark and wide and questioning her.

'There is no question of you leaving,' he said sternly.

'Don't you want to hear how all this has come about? My mother marrying Gio, the father of her daughter?'

Nina shrugged, surprising herself with her strength. But she had no choice but to shrug it away. She wasn't without pride, either. She'd tried to save her own face before now, so this last time shouldn't be much of an effort.

'It's nothing to do with me, Lorenzo,' she told him, quietly and sensibly. 'I understand now, though, your urgency in wanting to keep me out of the way. Your own mother is the woman Gio is marrying. It's natural you wouldn't want me around at such a sensitive time for everyone. All the more reason for me to go before she gets here.'

He grasped her arm as she went to turn back into the house. His fury bit into her arm and it stiffened Nina's resolve to get out of this with her chin up.

'You are going nowhere, Nina, not even inside to clean the house, which happens to be spotless anyway, until you explain yourself.'

Did he mean why she had been trying to trace Gio if she wasn't his lover? That hardly mattered any more, surely?

'Explain what? There's nothing to explain. I'm not stupid and nor are you. Work it out for yourself why I have to leave.'

His eyes blazed with rage and frustration. 'Well, I must be stupid because I can't see what you think is staring me in the face. Are you still mad at me for going to Gio for confirmation that you were never his lover? Can't you begin to understand my motivation in doing that? You had been making enquiries about him and, yes, I was wrong in presuming you were his mistress. It didn't take me long to realise you weren't that sort of woman anyway, but I still had to know if there was a connection between the two of you. And, yes, it is to do with my pride and my mother's pride. She's been through enough with Gio without having it all spoiled for her at the eleventh hour!'

'And that is exactly why I'm leaving,' Nina shot back at him. 'Because of your mother's eleventh hour! Best she never has sight of me, Lorenzo, and, yes, you are stupid for not working it out.' Oh, she had to do this. She hated herself for it but it was the only way. Once she had delivered her reasoning Lorenzo would wish he had never taken the trouble to rescue her from a Palermo gutter in the first place.

'You see, you *didn't* get confirmation from Gio that I was never his lover!' she scathed at him.

'And what is that supposed to mean?' he roared.

And Nina didn't even flinch at his anger. How could she when she was frozen inside? Her eyes met his with a steely determination to end this before his mother and his sister arrived to complicate matters more.

'You didn't get confirmation from Gio,' she repeated. 'What you got was a *lie*. And if you can't work that out I'll put you out of your misery once and for all.' She paused slightly to draw breath and to moisten her dry lips.

'Of course he denied all knowledge of me,' she reasoned determinedly. 'He's about to marry *your* mother. You might be close to Gio but you aren't that close where indiscretion is concerned. It's what any man would do so close to his wedding. Gio denied my very existence because I'm not important to him and Sofia is and, like you, he wants this wedding to go smoothly.'

His eyes darkened like storm clouds gathering. She had accused Gio of being a liar, and loyal Lorenzo Biacci didn't like that. But Nina had to go on.

'So now you know why I never denied it,' she went on, voice rising, eyes narrowed to emphasise what she was saying. 'Because it *happened*, Lorenzo. I *was* once

Gio's lover. We met in London, earlier this year, and, yes, we had a whirlwind affair which I obviously took more seriously than he did, but I didn't know that till I got here. And, yes, that is why I came to Sicily to look for him, and it's why you will now let me go. As you once said, I'm the last person any of you need around at a wedding! The damned mistress!'

She spun on her heel and stormed into the kitchen. The ice was gone now, replaced by the burning slush of hurt inside her. Now there was no going back. She'd said it all and he believed her.

The burning inside her flamed as she flew up the stone stairs to the bedroom. Lorenzo believed her! He had been stunned by her revelation, his eyes had completely blanked off from her in a last glacial look before she had spun out of his air space. And he hadn't come after her in a rage, demanding her to retract her admission. And—ridiculous, ridiculous—she had wanted him to!

She slammed the door of her bedroom behind her and leaned back on it. She was shaking now, and that treacherous unmade bed across the room seemed to be mocking her for being such a fool. And what a fool she was—a fool for loving him, a fool for allowing him to love her. A fool for ever coming to Sicily in the first place.

She shifted away from the door to pack her things. In her haste to smash all bridges between her and Lorenzo she hadn't given a thought to how she was going to get out of here, or what she would do or where to go. But now Lorenzo realised it was best there was distance between her and his mother he'd be only too willing to pay her for her services. It would kill her to have to ask for money, but there again he was probably already raiding his piggy bank in his haste to be shot of her!

And then she burst into tears because everything was

so insufferable. She loved him so much and she had destroyed it all, but it had been so necessary.

'Oh, no,' she suddenly moaned, her hands going to her mouth. She could hear something, a sound alien to any she had heard since arriving here. She knew all the sounds: the wind in the poplars, the buzz of cicadas, the creak of the old house as it settled for the night. But this sound, this throb of a car engine, far away but getting closer—oh, God, they were here. So soon. *Too* soon!

Nina ran to the window to see if the car had arrived, but it faced the wrong way. She knew that, of course, but in her panic had run there all the same. She twisted and turned in panic. What to do and where to run to? She was trapped. Nowhere to go. Think! Think! Think!

Carlo lay sleeping in the shade of the old olive tree. Nina sat cross-legged under the same tree, her sketchpad on her knees, her hands moving a sable-tipped brush mechanically over the page. She saw none of what she was doing; she was blind to it, deaf to any sound around her. How long she had been sitting here she didn't know, but a long time anyway. Her legs were cramped. She was thirsty and melting in the heat.

She couldn't really remember getting here, had only a vague recollection of scurrying down the stairs with her sketching materials clutched to her heaving breast. She had seen no one, heard nothing more. Her faithful friend had met her with love and devotion and now he slept at her feet, unaware of the anguish she was going through.

'Hello, you're Nina, aren't you?'

Nina's head shot up. Her eyes blinked against the brightness outside the shade of the tree she sat under. Her heart clenched.

Cristina! She was just like her photo. No mistake. She was dark and lovely, with long wavy chestnut hair that

flowed down her back—and so unlike Nina she wondered if it was possible that they were half-sisters at all.

Her mind flash-fired the thought that she had made a
huge mistake and this lovely girl wasn't her half-sister
and Gio Giulianni wasn't her real father. For a wild second or two she thought how wonderful if it were true
and she had no genetic link with these people whatsoever. But deep inside her the truth pulse throbbed. She
knew in her heart that Gio was her father—how, she
didn't know, just instinct, she supposed, just as she had
known Lorenzo was someone special in her life when
he had driven her out of Palermo that first morning.

Cristina was smiling, slightly hesitantly as you might
at someone you had never met before. Nina just stared
at her blankly, lost for words.

Carlo was suddenly aroused from his sleep by her
voice and leapt up, his tail wagging furiously, a guttural
sound of welcome rattling in his throat. He bounded
across his run to greet her.

Cristina laughed and opened the wire mesh gate and
sank to her knees to wrap her arms around the big dog,
regardless of the ankle-length flowing silk dress of lilac
and pink she wore that now trailed in the dust.

'Oh, darling Carlo. Have you missed me? I missed
you too, but Lorenzo said Nina has been looking after
you so I don't feel so bad for leaving you.' She grinned
and looked up at Nina, who had somehow managed to
get to her feet. 'Thank goodness you were here. They
hate each other. I don't know why, but perhaps it's a
clash of strong wills.'

She came towards Nina, across Carlo's dusty compound, holding out her hand. 'I'm Cristina, as if you
haven't guessed,' she laughed. 'Lorenzo has just been
telling us about you. It's all so funny.'

Nina insides clenched, but she managed to lift her
hand to take Cristina's. Just what had Lorenzo told

them? The truth? Hardly. He'd probably made up a pack of lies because the truth wouldn't do their Sicilian pride any good.

'I think it so romantic,' Cristina enthused, taking Nina's hand, her touch warm and friendly. 'Him stopping to pick you up from the street. You must tell me all about it. Were those people awful to you? I've never been to that part of Palermo. In fact I hardly know Sicily at all—not till this last year. I was brought up in America.'

Nina smiled. 'That accounts for no Italian accent,' she said softly, wondering what to say next. How exactly had Lorenzo explained her being here? She must be careful, very careful. Cristina was sweet, and the last thing she wanted to do was to hurt her.

'Um, how was your journey? Lorenzo said you'd been shopping in Milan.'

Cristina laughed and waved a small hand dismissively. 'Shopping was good, but Mamma enjoyed it more. She's so happy about the wedding, but I really don't know why they are bothering.' Cristina laughed again. 'Papà says it's only right, but I'm a different generation and it doesn't bother me one bit being illegitimate. Most of the girls at my boarding school had murky pasts. Oh, dear.' She sighed. 'I've shocked you, haven't I?'

Nina smiled nervously. If she only knew the shocks she had experienced since coming here! Illegitimacy was nothing. She'd lived with it herself all her life. But Cristina presumed she knew the whole story, which made her wonder again just how much Lorenzo had told them about her. It embarrassed her not to know. It made her cautious as to what to say to Cristina.

'Are you all right?' Christina asked with sudden concern. 'You look a little pale.'

'I've been sitting here with Carlo for too long,' she explained, with a smile to show she was just fine. 'I need

to stretch my legs.' She needed to get away. Somewhere
on her own because this was such a strange confronta-
tion, one that didn't make her feel at all at ease.

'Good idea,' Cristina enthused. 'We'll go for a walk.
Come on, Carlo, you can come too.'

Nina was about to protest when Cristina grinned at
her happily. 'Oh, Nina, I'm so glad you're here—someone of my own age to gossip with. Mamma is resting
and Lorenzo can be such a bore at times. Besides, he's
on the phone all the time and he said to look after you
and that's what I'm going to do.' She laughed. 'Oh, not
because *he* said so but because I want to. Come on. I've
got some cold drinks in my bag. Have you found the
secret path to the cove yet? Lorenzo wouldn't have
shown you. He never goes down there. It's where his
father died.'

She swung back towards the gate, Carlo gleefully
bounding ahead of her, and Nina stayed rooted to the
spot.

Cristina had taken her breath away, chilled her to the
marrow at what she had just said. Lorenzo's father had
died in the cove. Had he committed suicide over that
stone wall where she had strayed and he had come after
her, thinking she was about to leap over too? No, she
was being melodramatic, but it was hardly surprising;
she had been plunged into a Sicilian tragedy since arriving. She was getting as dramatic as everyone else.

Nina went to follow, not wanting to but sensing that
Cristina wouldn't accept no or some flimsy excuse like
a headache.

'Nina, darling, where are you going?'

Nina jumped at the gate as she was closing it behind
her. Lorenzo was coming towards her down the path that
led to Carlo's part of the garden. Cristina was way ahead
with Carlo, swinging her soft fabric bag at her side, her
flowing dress ruffling around her ankles, seeming to be

very happy back in Sicily. She turned as she heard
Lorenzo but didn't stop, just waved and carried on.

And he had only called her darling for Cristina's sake.
What lies had he told them?

'Where are you going?' he repeated—no 'darling' this
time.

'Just for a walk,' she told him stiffly. 'You instructed
Cristina to look after me and that's what she is doing.'

He caught her arm and drew her close to him. Nina
looked up at him in alarm, wondering what he was going
to do. He looked strained, she realised, his eyes expressionless, but the tautness of his features and the creamy
paleness of his skin said it all. He found the whole situation as embarrassing and as fraught as she did.

'Before you go, you say nothing to Cristina to alarm
her in any way,' he growled under his breath.

'Alarm her!' Nina echoed baldly. 'What do you think
I am, Lorenzo?'

'I know exactly what you are,' he bit back at her, eyes
dangerously black. 'I've told her and Mamma that we
met in Palermo by chance—'

'So I've heard,' Nina snapped, trying to get her arm
out of his vice-like lock. 'She thinks it highly amusing
but I don't. Just what did you tell them? Not the whole
truth, I bet?'

'Enough,' Lorenzo growled again, refusing to let her
go. He drew her closer to him till their noses were nearly
touching. His eyes were slivers of jet. 'They know that
you were evicted from the Locastos and why—toned
down, of course—'

'Oh, of course,' Nina grated sarcastically.

He shook her. 'Listen to me. I picked you up and
brought you back here because you had nowhere else to
go. You stayed and we are now having an affair—'

Nina drew in her breath with angry amazement.

'Yes, an affair!' he reiterated.

'It sounds cheap and sordid,' Nina protested hotly.

'Should suit you just fine, then, shouldn't it?'

Her eyes blazed. 'That was uncalled for—'

'It was exactly what you asked for,' he slammed back at her. 'You are the one claiming to be mistress material, so it should sit well on your shoulders for a while longer. Cristina and my mother believe you to be my lover and that is the way it is going to be from now on. To all eyes we are in love, do you understand? This is for my sister and my mother, and if you give them any reason to doubt it you will wish you had never been born.'

He let her go then and Nina staggered back, her eyes wide. At this moment in time she *did* wish she had never been born. What a dreadful pretence he was suggesting—for himself, not her. She *was* in love. It would be insufferable for her but she could see no other way out for them all. The truth wasn't a consideration and hadn't ever been, she thought miserably.

'And…and for how long do I have to act love's sweet dream?' she asked drily.

'For as long as I see fit. No doubt they will want to return to Palermo in a couple of days—'

'A couple of days?' Nina blurted. 'I have to pretend to *like* you that long?'

'Pretence is your middle name, Nina,' he said coldly. 'No trouble to you, but I'm the one who is going to suffer. My life is based on truth and honesty and lying is alien to me.'

'Yet you damned well do it all the time,' she accused violently. 'Especially in bed! You hypocrite!'

Suddenly he hauled her into his arms and his mouth exploded on hers. A kiss of such violence it shook her rigid. It scoured her mouth till it burned, and then it softened…softened to…love's sweet dream…and Nina knew just why. Over and above the thudding of her heart she heard a small laugh and the deep rumble of a growl down the pathway that led to the clifftop. Yes, a pretence for Cristina, who had obviously come back to see what was holding her up.

Lorenzo let her go. His voice was a deep whisper of warning. 'Keep this up, *darling*,' he grazed cynically, 'if you know what is good for you.' He pushed her away from him, but to onlookers it might have looked as if he was pushing her away because she was a temptation to him, and here and now wasn't the time or the place for anything more.

He grinned at her and then lifted his hand to stroke the side of her face lovingly. Oh, what a damned actor he was. 'Now off you go,' he whispered, as if talking to a child. 'Go and play with Cristina.' A dark brow rose cynically. 'Talk your girly-talk, but be very careful what you say and how you say it.' He frowned suddenly. 'Funny, but I think you will get along like a house on fire. You share a lot of similarities—gaucheness, naivety, innocence. But of course yours isn't genuine, is it?'

'Go to blazes!' Nina whispered under her breath, and then she smiled, the smile of one covering hurt with trickery. She leaned forward and kissed his cheek lightly. 'See you later, darling,' she said, loud enough for Cristina to hear, but for Lorenzo's ears only she added frostily, 'At the gates of hell, Lorenzo Biacci!'

'I'm so happy for Lorenzo,' Cristina enthused as Nina caught her up at last. 'I never thought he'd meet anyone suited to him. He's had lots of girlfriends but no one serious. Mamma thinks it's because of our background. He's seen what a mess they have made with their lives and is wary of love and marriage. He takes life far too seriously.'

Yes, honourable Lorenzo Biacci, born out of his own generation, Nina thought dejectedly. It didn't surprise her to hear confirmation from someone else that he was so stiff-upper-lipped, so self-righteous, so pompous. And

yet this morning he had loved her so deeply and unconditionally, and she so naively had thought he had put
aside what he'd believed—that she had once been Gio's
mistress.

And if that had been true she could almost have ad-
mired him for the effort and inward turmoil he had con-
quered in the name of love. But it *hadn't* been the way
it had appeared. He had had to check with Gio first!

She bit her lip as she followed Cristina down the narrow path. He had said he had realised she wasn't the
sort, but still he had gone to Gio. Another snippet of
their row came back to her. He had said he had wanted
to know if there was any connection between them. That
would have been dangerous if he had dug deeper, but of
course Gio didn't know who she was.

Had he ever known of her existence? she wondered,
not for the first time. Had her mother concealed her preg-
nancy from him? Had their affair been so brief that his
opinion of the decision to put her up for adoption hadn't
been sought? They were all questions she had wanted to
ask him when they met, to somehow fill that void in her
past, but that was an impossibility now. It was an un-
bidden thought but one she couldn't help. She felt
cheated. But it was her own fault. If she hadn't fallen in
love with Lorenzo... No, even that wasn't good reasoning. It would have been better if she had never met him
in the first place!

'Lorenzo said you were very bubbly but I don't think
you are.' Cristina had stopped by the stone wall over-
looking the sea. She smiled at Nina. 'You've hardly said
a word.'

Nina smiled at her, thinking that there were probably
more years between them than she and Lorenzo had sur-
mised. Or perhaps since coming here Nina had aged a
thousand years!

'You've done all the talking so far, Cristina,' she told

her. 'Not that I'm complaining,' she added with a wider grin. 'It's nice to talk to someone who's lived in America. Tell me about it. I've always wanted to go there.' Best to keep on neutral ground, she thought as Cristina laughed and headed along the clifftop path where Nina took Carlo for long runs to clear her head.

Cristina talked non-stop about living in New York and being shipped off to Switzerland for her schooling. There had been holidays in the Caribbean and the Seychelles, and cruises. All in all it sounded as if Cristina had had a very affluent upbringing, considering she hadn't come from a stable parental relationship.

'We weren't allowed to come to Sicily for holidays,' Cristina gabbled on. 'Gio was still married, though Mamma used to slip over now and then to see her sisters, and Gio, of course. Gio used to come to us in New York, four or five times a year, so he's always been my Papà. Look, here are the steps. You don't have vertigo or anything, do you? They are very steep—be careful.'

She went ahead, pushing back thick dry grass three feet high to find the steps, gathering her floaty skirt around her knees. Nina followed, deciding she didn't suffer from vertigo—only when Lorenzo had been holding her back from the precipice. His very touch had made her head spin.

And her head was spinning now, and nothing to do with the steepness of the steps. She was beginning to work it all out. Gio had been married when he had had an affair with Sofia and conceived Cristina. Had he also been married when he had had an affair with her own mother? She was older than Cristina, only a few years, so perhaps if he'd been married that could explain why she had been given up for adoption.

They finally reached the small cove below and Cristina flung herself down on the warm yellow sand and rummaged in her bag. Carlo flew down to the water's edge and ran like mad, snapping at the salt water and then flinging his head from side to side with distaste.

'Silly dog,' Cristina laughed. 'Now his bandage is all wet. What happened to his paw? Here, have a drink. Isn't it lovely here?'

Nina sank down next to her and took the can she offered. She told her about Carlo's thorn and how Lorenzo had removed it—was it only yesterday?

'Gosh, I'm amazed Carlo let him do that. But Lorenzo said how close you two were, and dogs know these things, don't they?'

Nina nodded and wondered if she meant she and Lorenzo were close or she and Carlo, but it didn't really matter. She sighed as she gazed out to sea. She had wanted to steer Cristina away from personal issues, keep to talking about her life in New York, but that didn't seem to matter any more either. Even when the girl talked of her childhood she let slip tantalising titbits that involved Gio and her mother. She burned to know more about Gio and Sofia and his marriage, and Lorenzo, and how they all slotted into each other's lives like a jigsaw. A jigsaw with a picture that she, Nina, didn't have in front of her to work from.

'So I presume that Gio is divorced now and free to marry your mother?' Nina started cagily.

'Oh, hasn't Lorenzo told you the history of it all?' Cristina said with a small frown. Then she laughed softly. 'I suppose you've been so wrapped up with each other there hasn't been much time.' She lay back in the sand, linked her bare arms behind her head and closed her eyes. 'It's all so romantic, you and Lorenzo. He's absolutely besotted with you. Mamma is so excited and can't wait to meet you. She's cooking supper tonight so you'll meet her then.'

Nina sat stiff and cross-legged next to Cristina, disappointed that she appeared to be falling asleep and she wasn't going to find out anything more. She gazed out to sea and along the small cove to the rocks that appeared to have been tossed down from the clifftop above, or had been erupted up from some prehistoric volcano. Her own feelings were erupting like Etna once had.

Lorenzo besotted with her? What a lie. How cruel of him to make it all the worse. It would have been better if he had agreed with her that her presence wasn't wanted and, instead of cooking up a hotpot of lies, banished her there and then so she wouldn't have to suffer a supper with the wedding family. But perhaps this was his punishment to her—a parting gift for the mistress!

'Papà's wife died last year,' Cristina murmured. 'She had been ill for some time so it wasn't a great shock. According to Papà, she always seemed to have some ailment or other, right from when they were first married. He shouldn't have married her in the first place. Papà has always admitted that. He married in haste but he tried to make the best of it. They have big families out here and Papà wanted children, but she always made some excuse.'

Didn't stop Gio making babies elsewhere, Nina thought uncharitably.

Suddenly Cristina rolled over to face Nina, who was digging her fingers into the sand for pebbles to dash against the nearest rock.

'My Papà is wonderful,' she told Nina sincerely, her dark eyes glowing with love for him. 'He's just about the cleverest banker in Sicily. He's very respected, but that's usually the sort who fall down badly where their private lives are concerned.'

Nina turned her head and looked deeply at Cristina. 'I don't think you had better say any more, Cristina.' She lowered her eyes. 'Lorenzo wouldn't like it—'

'Lorenzo adores Gio and you're going to be a part of

the family anyway,' Cristina laughed. 'Anything I tell you you'll know soon enough.'

Nina couldn't help a cynical smile faltering at her lips. *Her* a part of the family? The more she heard from Cristina the more distanced she was becoming. She was now being downgraded to the result of a one-night stand, slotted in somewhere between Gio's unhappy marriage and a long-standing affair with Lorenzo's mother.

Cristina was sitting upright now, and gazing out to the same sea Nina was gazing blindly at.

'Papà and Mamma practically grew up together, but they were never lovers. Papà was too busy learning the family business. Mamma married Romano Biacci. She was very young. Too young, I think—eighteen. It was what they did in those days. Papà said he didn't know how deeply he cared for Mamma till her wedding day. He saw her on the arm of Romano and it suddenly hit him what he had lost. But it was too late.'

Cristina suddenly sighed. 'Papà told me all this because he said it might help me not to get myself in such a mess where the heart was concerned. Mamma was happy, though, unaware of how Papà really felt about her. She lived here; this is the family home. Lorenzo was born here. Papà was in Palermo, working and building up his future and trying to forget Mamma and then a few years later—Lorenzo was about eight then—Papà fell in love again.'

'And married her quickly to make sure this time,' Nina offered quietly, wondering where her own mother had fitted into Gio's life. *Had* she been his lover during a difficult marriage with a wife who was ailing all the time?

'No, he didn't marry that one.' Cristina smiled. 'He loved her very much, though. For a time she filled his life. Mamma knew her and liked her and she was happy for Gio. She wasn't Sicilian, though, and that makes an enormous difference. It did then anyway, in their generation. Papà's family were dead against her. She worked for another banking family in Palermo, as an au pair, and they didn't consider her good enough for Gio.' Cristina suddenly laughed. 'You see how things have changed. You were an au pair and met Lorenzo and fell in love and Mamma is happy for you both, and when Gio hears he will be delighted too.'

Nina couldn't summon a smile at the coincidence of that. Her heart was beating so rapidly it was chilling the blood in her veins. She felt sick with what she was working out in her mind.

'Wa—was she English?' Nina asked faintly. Was Cristina, unknowingly, telling her about her own mother? Nina knew nothing about her. Her adoptive parents had known nothing about her either, or if they had they hadn't told her, only that she had died when she was tiny.

'Yes. Papà says she was so beautiful, so different from any of the Sicilian women he had met. He was determined to marry her, but the family…' She sighed. 'Oh, it was so tragic.'

Nina crunched pebbles in the palm of her damp hand. She didn't want to hear more and yet she did. She wanted to know and yet she didn't. She felt so hot and faint, and tried so hard not to show Cristina how desperate she felt.

'W-what was so tragic?' she murmured, to prompt Cristina, who had suddenly grown quiet.

Cristina gave a small shrug of her bare shoulders. She looked sad, and Nina wished she hadn't prompted her.

'I suppose I wouldn't be here now…' she mused, and took a short breath. 'If they had married and the baby had lived…'

Nina felt as if she had been punched in the stomach. 'She was pregnant, you see, and Gio was so happy because his family would have to consent to their marriage. But instead they made her return to England. Gio didn't know this till after, when it was too late to go and get her back. He just thought she had wanted to go back home to think things over. Then she wrote to say…to say she had lost the baby and now she was back in England she had decided they weren't suited at all. Gio was devastated and never really got over it, and then he married a Sicilian woman—on the rebound, I suppose—and that was a disaster, and…'

She paused to draw breath again and Nina held hers tightly in her throat, unable to respond to anything more Cristina was saying. She was listening through a tunnel of pain. Her mother had lied to Gio. She hadn't lost the baby at all. The pressure from his family and realising that she would never fit into their proud lives had forced her to lie. She had had her baby, had put her up for adoption because she couldn't cope and perhaps hadn't had anyone back in England to turn to. Oh, it *was* tragic, so very sad. And she, Nina Parker, was the living proof of that tragedy.

'Mamma was always there for him, though,' Cristina was telling her. 'Only as friends, of course—just as he was there for her, when Lorenzo's father died. Here in this cove. He was swimming and apparently had a heart attack and drowned. It was such a shock for Mamma because he was so young, and you don't expect that sort of thing to happen.'

She took a long breath and gathered her arms around her shoulders. 'Mamma and Papà grew closer and really fell in love then, and…' She suddenly grinned at Nina. 'Then Mamma was pregnant with me. Can you imagine the difficulties that caused?'

Numbly Nina nodded. Given the proud temperament of these people, and their not wanting a scandal, she could well understand.

'Papà always stood by her, though, and looked after her. A divorce from his own wife was out of the question. Papà took Mamma to America and set her up there, and has lived a double life ever since. When you're as rich as Croesus you can do that.' She giggled and then went on. 'Lorenzo came back when he finished his studies. Papà had always looked after the Biacci estate for him, but Lorenzo didn't settle too well and came back to America.' She sighed suddenly. 'I don't know what is going to happen after the wedding, where we will all settle. Papà is Sicilian through and through and I suspect Mamma will want to stay. I don't know about Lorenzo. Have you talked about where you will live when you are married?'

Stunned, Nina parted her lips with shock. More lies, more pretence to keep everyone sweet for this wedding? Had Lorenzo told them they were going to be married?

Suddenly she didn't want to hear any more, or even open her mouth to say anything that might incriminate herself. She wanted to be on her own, to mull over all that she had learned. She had a huge weight of sadness inside her.

'Oh, look at Carlo,' she forced out, getting to her feet. 'His bandage has come loose and it's tangled in his other leg. I'll rescue him. You go on back and I'll catch you up.'

Cristina was already on her feet. 'Yes, I'd better get back. I've loads of unpacking to do. Nina!' she called out as Nina started to drag her feet through the sand towards Carlo, who was whining with impatience at the tangle he had got himself into.

Nina turned. Cristina was smiling happily. 'It's lovely to have you here. Later you must tell me all about your life. I've been so selfish, telling you all about mine.' She laughed. 'But I bet you haven't any skeletons rattling in your cupboard,' she joked.

You'll never know, Nina said to herself as she managed to lift a leaden hand to wave her goodbye.

Nina sank to her knees in the damp sand at the edge of the water and with trembling hands freed Carlo, who thanked her with a wet nuzzle against her face. Nina clamped her arms around his neck and buried her hot face in his wet fur and cried and cried. She cried for the mother she had never known, who had lied to protect herself from more hurt, for Gio who had never known she had even been born, and she cried for her and Lorenzo because their love was evermore impossible now.

'Oh, Carlo,' she sobbed. 'I shouldn't have come to Sicily. It was…was the worst decision of my life!'

CHAPTER NINE

LATER Nina went back to the house, dragging her heels, not wanting to be there. But it seemed there was no escape for the time being. She was going to have to face them all at supper time and already the tension was piling up on more tension inside her.

There was no hope for her and Lorenzo, she thought miserably as she climbed the terrace steps, brushing her windswept hair from her deathly pale face. She loved him so much and for a brief while she had been so happy, but how could she reveal herself now? Gio had never known she had been born. If he truly had loved her mother it would tear him apart to know now. It might change how he felt for Sofia and he was on the threshold of marrying her after what sounded like a deep, long relationship that must have been fraught with problems from the start.

The alternative was to give her love to Lorenzo, bury her secret in the darkest crevice of her being and live with it to save the happiness of others. Did she have the strength to do that? Because it would take strength—a huge amount—living a lie, denying what she had wanted most in her life: the love of a real father.

But, even if she took that enormous step, how was she going to explain to Lorenzo just why she had been looking for Gio in the first place? She'd have to go back on her admittance that Gio had been her lover and...

She sighed fretfully. Why was she giving herself all this angst anyway? Lorenzo believed that she had been Gio's mistress and all this nonsense about her and

Lorenzo being lovers was but a show for Sofia and Cristina, just for long enough till he'd thought of a way of easing her out of all their lives without any trouble. As he had proposed to do from the very start.

There was no one in the kitchen and Nina stood for a while, ears alert to the smallest sound. There was utter silence, and she guessed they were all still resting in the heat of the late afternoon.

And Nina desperately wanted to lie down herself. Her mind was exhausted and her body ached as a result of digesting all that Cristina had told her, leaving her with a dulling sadness. There could never be a place for her in this close-knit family, and after all this heartache she would never meet her father anyway.

And Lorenzo? It was the hugest pain of all to endure. She had found her love and lost it because his hadn't been given to her willingly. Briefly he had possessed her, but only because she had offered it so easily.

Nina gasped as she opened her bedroom door and quickly closed it quietly again. Cristina was sprawled on her bed, sound asleep, and the room was littered with luggage and glossy designer carrier bags.

'Shh.'

Nina nearly jumped out of her skin as Lorenzo cupped a cool hand on her elbow and guided her back down the white walled passageway. He opened another door and urged her inside, closing the door soundlessly behind them.

'That was Cristina's room before you came and I've moved you into mine now,' he told her quietly. 'It's what everyone expects.'

Nina's mouth gaped open with shock, but almost immediately snapped shut to a thin line of defiance. From the corner of her eye she saw the huge double bed that languished mockingly against the far wall. No doubt he would milk this situation for all it was worth and expect her to share it with him! She wrenched her elbow from his hand and spun to face him angrily, her face flushed, her heart hurting.

'No one expects anything of the sort!' she blazed. 'There are plenty more bedrooms here and you are just doing this to hurt me, to punish me for ever coming to Sicily to rock your lives. I'm not having any of it, Lorenzo,' she added heatedly. 'I'm not sharing that bed with you. No way.'

'You will,' he told her coolly. 'But don't push your luck that anything will happen in it apart from sleep, of course—'

'Push my luck?' Nina cried incredulously. 'Your ego astounds me! But there again, it shouldn't. After what I've just heard about you and your family...' She checked herself immediately, eyes blinking rapidly as she lowered her head away from him. Damn, she musn't let her anger and hurt force her into saying something she couldn't get out of later. She swung away from him. 'Where are my things?' she asked him weakly.

'All put away neatly,' he told her quietly. 'What has Cristina been telling you about the family?'

Nina didn't answer because she couldn't. It was all getting too much for her. She felt so weak and ineffectual against him. She crossed the room, pulled open a drawer and saw all his underwear neatly stacked. She slammed it shut quickly, tears burning her eyes.

'What has she been telling you?' he repeated.

He made no attempt to cross the room to her, and she was grateful for that at the very least. Distance between them was what she demanded. Closeness she wouldn't be able to endure. She might crumble in his arms and lose control. She opened another drawer and found her own things and pulled fresh underwear from it before sliding it shut with a thud.

'The family history,' she mumbled.

There was a long silence, almost intimidating her to fill it, but she resisted by biting her lower lip hard.

'It isn't a very pretty story, is it?' he said softly.

'I'd say that was the understatement of the year.' She mumbled again. Her clean underwear clutched in her hands, she leaned against the chest of drawers for support. She didn't want to be reminded of it. It hurt too much.

'Has it hurt you?' Lorenzo asked, as if he was aware of the pain she was suffering.

He couldn't know exactly why, but it was something to latch onto for the time being. Slowly she turned and faced him, brave again.

'It saddened me, Lorenzo,' she said softly, her eyes misted. 'No one could escape being moved by hearing such a tragedy. And that is why I shall do as you bid and play your little game for you tonight. Yes, I'll pretend to be your lover, but only for this evening, in front of your mother and Cristina, and then tomorrow you will make arrangements for me to leave and it's up to you what you tell them. You've made up enough lies about our relationship, so another shouldn't hurt you too much.'

'I've told you, lying is alien to me.'

'I think not!' she objected as she hauled open the wardrobe and rummaged for the only dress she had—a white cotton sundress that would have to do for this evening. She pulled it out before slamming the door shut again. 'You told Cristina we were going to be married, and that is an outrageous bending of the truth.'

'I said nothing of the sort to Cristina or my mother,' he said soberly.

Nina's heart plummeted as he denied it. Ridiculous. Why should she be hurt when she should have expected it?

She heard his step on the polished oak floor behind her and swung round to face him, her back stiff against the panelling of the wardrobe. 'Cristina said we were going to be married,' she said hurriedly, 'and she must have got that from you because I'm certainly not under any illusions about our relationship!'

'She *supposed*,' Lorenzo corrected, dark hypnotic eyes seeking hers to trap them. 'I told you she was an innocent. She believes that if two people are having an affair such as ours it naturally progresses to marriage.'

Nina spluttered out a self-protective laugh. 'She supposes nothing of the kind! She wonders why her mother and father are bothering with this marriage after their long and troubled affair. She's a very liberated young lady.'

Lorenzo shook his head. 'Whatever Cristina has told you about her mother and Gio, however flippant she may have sounded, it is all to cover her own feelings. She's as desperate for this marriage as all of us. She's lived with a part-time father all her life and now it is all coming right for her.'

Desperately Nina tried to hold back her tears for Cristina. She understood more than Lorenzo could ever know. Her heart went out to the sweet girl and she tried not to think of her own despair. To come so close to finding where her own heart lay only to have it broken because others had more right than she deserved.

She had found her own father; she would never meet him but at least she knew all about him now. But, worse, she had found the man she loved more than anything else in the world, and even that was denied her because of this tangled web of tragedy she had become unwittingly embroiled in.

Twisting her underwear in her hands, she gazed at Lorenzo in utter defeat.

'All the more reason for me to go,' she whispered softly, her eyes pleading with his to make it easy for her. Make him agree, make him lose his temper, even, and throw the mistress scenario at her for the last time and be done with it. 'I now understand the importance of this wedding, Lorenzo,' she went on, 'more than I ever did before meeting Cristina. I can't face her again and it would be embarrassing to meet your mother, and…and it's best that I go. I have a history with Gio, one…one that I'm not proud of, and it would be wrong of me to stay a minute longer.'

He stepped closer to her, a dark, menacing threat to her heart. Her whole body seized in anticipation of him laying his hands on her. Mercifully he stopped a foot away from her, close enough for her to breathe his heat, which sent her blood rushing, but not close enough for her to let her reserve completely shatter.

She moistened her dry lips. 'Please, Lorenzo. Don't put us all through this—'

'You are staying because I want to make everyone happy,' he threw at her, eyes dark and defying her to argue.

'H-happiness is a God-given gift,' she stammered, 'not yours to fool around with!'

He lifted his hand and cupped her chin, and because it felt stiff and cold and not warm and persuasive she knew she had a chance. And she would play it for all it was worth.

She jerked her chin out of his grasp but there was no escape; her back was hard up against the wardrobe.

'If…if you make me stay,' she hissed through her

teeth, 'I can't be responsible for what...I might let slip. You can't afford to take that chance. I...I'm a danger to you all. Over dinner there could be questions I can't answer. I...might get muddled. I might get drunk. I might blurt it all out and—'

He grasped her angrily by the shoulders and pulled her hard against him. 'Force yourself to damn well lie, then, as you are so quick to accuse others of doing!'

Oh, how she had stabbed at his loyalty when she had accused Gio of lying.

His eyes were dark and accusing. 'And it shouldn't be too much trouble for you to do that yet again. To act the innocent with your wide eyes and appealing virginal looks. But what an act! I could almost believe that you were indeed Gio's lover but for one thing.' His hands seared into her flesh. 'I made love to you this very morning, and I didn't make love to someone else's mistress!' he ground out through white lips. 'You were good, but you couldn't disguise that one sharp intake of breath, the slight tensing of your body, anticipating pain. I was your first, Nina, and at the time it filled me with joy. But now, now it disgusts me.'

'Dis—disgusts you?' Nina faltered, nearly passing out with what he was saying; he was getting so close to thrashing the truth out of her. But disgust? She didn't understand that.

'Yes, disgust.' His eyes were narrowed and black with anger. 'Gio obviously didn't give you what you wanted when you met. But you didn't give up. You wanted him so badly you pursued him here to Sicily.'

Nina struggled so hard she heard his breath lock in his throat as he tried to control her. She beat her small fists on his hard chest and twisted her body violently to be free of him. Her throat burned with fury, tears flooded her eyes.

'I...I hate you for that!' she sobbed. 'I hate—'

He held her strongly, almost shaking her. 'You damn well don't, and well you know it. You love me as deeply as I love you and—'

And then all her fury and strength collapsed inside her like a pyramid of cards, fluttering down and down till she was but an inanimate heap in front of him. Weak and senseless, she felt his hand lift her chin, forcing her head up to meet his eyes.

'Why, Nina?' he breathed roughly, his voice throbbing with effort. 'Why accuse Gio of being a liar when you are the one not telling the truth? Why make me rage at you to try and break you when all I want to do is hold you in my arms and make love to you for ever? Why, for God's sake? Why are you putting us both through this agony?'

Because the truth would hurt too many people! she wanted to scream at him.

His eyes searched hers and then with a long, deep sigh he lowered his lips to her mouth. Nina caught a raw sob in her throat and held it there. Her eyes flickered shut as his magic swept through her weak and ineffectual body till she was limp in his arms. But treacherously not weak enough to be unaware of the fire still burning in her heart for him.

The kiss deepened dangerously, the heat of their harsh words to each other fanning the embers of a passion they had met full on earlier in the day. Once hadn't been enough. It had simply been the prologue to a life of passion and love with him, but she was being forced to cast it carelessly away from them both.

And she didn't want to but it was impossible, and then he was being impossible by pressing his hard body purposefully against her, and she felt the power and the arousal she hadn't the strength to resist, but she tried.

She tore her mouth from his and a feeble, plaintive, heart-torn, '*No,*' fell from her lips like a doomed snow-flake fluttering on fire. A hand on her chin forced her mouth back to his, the other slid up under her thin shirt, hot and demanding on her sensitive skin, caressing her back as he relentlessly plundered her mouth.

Her loins ached for him as he moved temptingly against her, his arousal grinding her resistance down till she started to tremble with longing for him.

'I'm going to make love to you, Nina,' he murmured throatily, 'because it's the only way to get the truth from you.' He swept her up into his arms and threw her down on the bed.

And dumbly Nina lay coiled there, watching him wide-eyed as he tore off his shirt and chinos, eyes never leaving hers, dark and determined. What truth was he seeking? That she loved him? What more proof did he need? But if he meant the truth about Gio, he hadn't a chance. He was already halfway there, knowing they had never been lovers, and now she understood that bitter accusation he had just thrown at her—that she hadn't got what she had wanted from Gio, hence her pursuing him across the continent. He was going for the final break that he thought would have her admitting just why she had come this far to find Gio Giulianni. But the truth would break *him*, and everyone else concerned.

She sprang up from the bed, but got no further than putting her feet on the rug next to it. She was hauled back and Lorenzo was over her, holding her flaying arms above her head. She expected his eyes to sear her flesh with anger at her defiance, but what she got was a deep, deep, heartfelt look of sheer despair.

'For God's sake, Nina, stop this, I beg you,' he pleaded. 'I can't bear your pain nor mine.'

He lowered his mouth tenderly to hers, and because

of the depth of warmth, not anger, it made it all worse for her. In their combined rage she had a chance against him, but in sensitivity she was lost. Her pulses throbbed, her bones weakened. There was no more fight in her, only a deep, deep longing to give herself completely and pray that a miracle might happen and when it was over all her troubles would have been lifted and blown away like morning mist.

She clung to him, arms wrapped tightly around him, her body yielding to his charisma. The kisses went on and on, and tenderly he moved her skirt aside, caressed her thighs, sliding his hand under her tiny briefs till she moaned ecstatically against his lips.

Her breasts swelled and ached as he cupped them and lowered his lips to draw sweetly on her raging nipples. Running her fingers through his coiled hair, she gasped and threw her head back against the pillow as he moved down to her stomach and lower still, till her head swam.

She arched against him, naked now, so dizzy with feeling she had hardly felt him dispose of her clothes.

She moaned his name as his mouth came back to hers, hot and scented, drawing on her lips. He pressed himself hard between her thighs. Her legs wrapped around him, drawing him in, and his breath locked in his throat as deeply and urgently he penetrated her so fully and thoroughly she was lost for ever.

Nina awoke later, aching in the aftermath of their love-making, and very much alone.

An evening breeze through the shutters temporarily cooled her brow as she blinked herself fully awake in the candlelit bedroom. It was nearly dark outside. She lay still for a few moments more and knew what she must do. It was hardly a miracle, but the mists in her head had cleared.

Her love for Lorenzo couldn't be denied—his for her neither. She remembered him kissing her brow and telling her how much he loved her before she had slipped into an exhausted sleep. No, she couldn't give him up, but she would have to sacrifice something else very special to her heart.

No one would ever know she was Gio's daughter. She would bury her deep, dark secret and live with it. To lose Lorenzo would be unbearable; to lose a father she had never had in the first place was a sacrifice she was now willing to make.

Nina showered, and dressed very carefully after washing her flaxen hair and drying it till it gleamed like melted butter. She put on a little make-up, mascara and lipstick, which brightened her pallor, though she was slightly tanned anyway—but her anguish lately had seemed to fade it. Around her neck she wore the only jewellery she had, the clear glass beads cut to look like crystal that she'd had bought in a Palermo market to cheer herself and that ghastly room at the Locastos.

She smiled, remembering how it had clinked in the gutter on that dreadful…no, wonderful day.

Satisfied that she had done her very best to look nice for everyone, she finally wandered around Lorenzo's bedroom, touching his things and pressing his clothes to her lips. It helped to calm her before the first trying test of her resolve to bury her past.

She took one last look at herself in a gilded mirror on the wall and smiled and lifted her chin. She could do it; she *would* do it. Her sincere love for Lorenzo and his for her was all the strength she needed. And if ever Lorenzo… The smile drooped slightly. If ever he wanted to know just why she had been looking for Gio… She lifted her chin again. Then she would pray for a miracle to help her through, because for the time being she couldn't think of one plausible reason that might satisfy his curiosity.

'You look lovely, Nina,' Lorenzo breathed at the foot of the stone stairs. He had been waiting for her, she realised, and she was pleased at his thoughtfulness. He looked wonderful in a lightweight white jacket, a white shirt and a rather formal black bow tie at his throat. His trousers were long and lean, formal black too, and Nina's heart sank to think she wasn't appropriately dressed.

She smiled hesitantly, and he took her hand and lifted it to his mouth to press a warm kiss on it, and then stepped back to murmur, 'How I always want you—radiant.' Then he smiled. 'Take courage. Sofia is as nervous of meeting you as you are of her, but she will adore you as I do.'

'I hope so,' Nina whispered, her eyes brimming with happiness as she clung to his arm. 'But I'm not really nervous—well, only a trifle—but if she's anything like Cristina then I have no worries.'

'There you two are,' Cristina suddenly called out as she skipped down the stairs behind them. 'I've been banging on your door for ever. I slept and slept. Oh, Nina, you look so different, so special. Have you met Mamma yet?'

'She's in the dining hall,' Lorenzo told her as Cristina veered off towards the kitchen, wearing the pale blue silk dress Lorenzo had offered to Nina when she had arrived. 'Putting the final touches to the table that you were supposed to have done,' Lorenzo lightly reprimanded her.

Laughing, Cristina altered her course and headed across the reception hall. 'It wouldn't have hurt you to have given her a hand—'

'I did,' Lorenzo laughed. 'Ready?' he directed to

Nina, his eyes glittering, his features far more relaxed than they had been for a long time.

Nina nodded, feeling almost light-headed at the joking warmth between Lorenzo and Cristina. It was going to be all right, she thought happily. She had made the right decision, to keep her secret bound inside her, and it was going to be all right.

Sofia was at the huge antique mahogany sideboard that Nina had always enjoyed polishing to perfection since she had been here. Her back was to them as she arranged silver cutlery, but, hearing them, she turned with a wide smile on her lovely face. And then her lips suddenly set like stone.

It was only a fleeting sensation, a very slight look of apprehension in Sofia's expression, but it was one that Nina didn't miss. She quickly supposed that she was being hypersensitive, because she had got the impression that Sofia had looked surprised at the sight of her.

Nina gazed at her, desperately searching her dark, liquid brown eyes for approval. She had expected Lorenzo's mother to be beautiful and she wasn't disappointed. She wondered if Sofia was searching for the same thing in this, their first sight of each other, hence her sudden look of apprehension.

But it was over in a second and Sofia was stepping towards her, very much an older version of the lovely Cristina, her hair shorter but the same glossy dark brown with only a trace of pale grey at her temples. She was slim and elegant and dressed in dark burgundy silk with a fine gold chain and crucifix at her throat which she fingered as she came to a stop in front of Nina.

'How lovely to meet you, Nina,' she whispered as she leaned forward to kiss Nina on each cheek.

Nina was touched to feel the hands on her upper arms tremble slightly at their contact with her. And as Sofia let her go she turned away from her rather abruptly and flashed Lorenzo a strange look that Nina was unable to interpret and that Lorenzo missed because he was gazing at *her* in rapt adoration, not at his mother.

Lorenzo's voice filled the room but Nina didn't know what he was saying; she was only aware of a silent atmosphere in the long, elegant dining room, lit by hundreds of candles in iron holders dotted around. It stressed her enormously.

Sofia didn't approve of her. Sofia was wondering what on earth her sleek, sophisticated lawyer son was doing with a sun-dressed flaxen-haired slip of a girl he had picked up in a Palermo gutter!

She felt small and under-dressed, undesirable and lacking against Sofia's elegance...she felt out of place...undermined...

Cristina was suddenly in the room, hugging her and laughing. 'Isn't she lovely, Mamma? I don't know what she sees in Lorenzo, though.'

There was a quick, light-hearted exchange of words between Cristina and Lorenzo, and then they were laughing, and Nina caught Sofia's eyes across the wide baronial dining table and her heart swelled, dispelling all her doubts that Sofia was disapproving of her. She was smiling, a warm smile, and her eyes glittered slightly. Nina wondered if it was tears, and then she heard Sofia murmur, 'Yes, she is very lovely and I'm happy for both of them.'

They sat down to pale green avocado mousse as a starter. Lorenzo poured wine, and then everyone seemed to be talking at once and Nina relaxed and supposed the tension in her own being had made her imagine all sorts of atmospheres that weren't there.

It was a delightful evening, light-hearted and warm, and occasionally Nina drew back from it all, at peace with herself, knowing that she could keep her secret— because amongst such lovely people how could she do otherwise? Little was said of the wedding, as if it was all arranged and nothing more needed to be said until closer to the day—which Nina was only slightly alarmed to hear was only a week off.

Lorenzo gave another hilarious account of how he and Nina had met, embellishing it even more this second time around, making it sound like a farce and making Nina realise just what a farce it had been. She was almost grateful for the Locastos' treatment of her, which had resulted in her meeting this wonderful man.

And in the early hours of the morning, after she had helped Sofia and Cristina clear up, she and Lorenzo, hugging each other tightly, crept up to bed while his mother and sister stayed up, talking softly on the warm terrace together.

Lorenzo made love to her, beautifully and lovingly, and later she coiled herself around him and slept peacefully. Happy and belonging.

Nina crept downstairs in the morning, the first up. Dressed in the white sun-dress she had worn the night before, so as not to disturb Lorenzo by opening drawers and cupboards, she opened the back door onto the terrace and breathed the warm, scented air.

She was deliciously happy, more than she had ever been in her life, and she wanted to share her happiness.

She ran all the way down to Carlo's compound. He greeted her with his usual exuberance, his paws leaving dusty marks on her white dress which Nina laughingly brushed off, reprimanding him playfully.

'Oh, Carlo, look what you've done to my sketchpad as well. Have you been sleeping on it all night?' She'd forgotten it yesterday, when Cristina had arrived to introduce herself. She picked it up, dusted it down and tucked it under her arm as she followed Carlo out of his run.

'Hey, wait for me!' she called out as he hurtled down the path through the gardens that led to the cliffs.

Nina was hot and breathless by the time she reached the rough stone wall. She leaned on it to catch her breath and drink in the spectacular view of the crystal blue sea frothing at the edges below in the cove. Nothing had looked more beautiful.

Carlo spotted a rabbit and flew like the wind after it, and Nina laughingly called out, 'No chance, Carlo, you've grown fat since I've been looking after you.'

Still laughing, she lifted her hands to push her hair back from her face for the wind to cool her brow. Her sketchpad slid from under her arm.

It never reached the ground.

Nina gasped with fright. And then her insides clenched fiercely as she jerked around to face…Gio Giulianni.

Her heart stopped. The world stopped. The wind on her flushed face suddenly chilled her like ice.

'Don't be afraid,' he murmured, his voice deep, his dark, dark eyes seeming to pierce through to her very soul. He held her sketchpad in one hand.

Nina's first thought was flight. To run and run till she dropped—because how could she ever have expected to get away with this charade she had talked herself into? To keep a secret such as hers once she was face to face with her very own father? But run she couldn't: her body was suddenly leaden, preparing itself to turn to stone.

She was facing her father for the first time in her life. Oh, God, this dark, handsome, strikingly powerful man was her father. Her eyes ate him up, devoured every crease and line and feature of his face, searching for something, anything that would compare to her own pale, delicate features. They were so very different.

He lifted his hand to give her back her sketchpad and Nina feverishly lowered her eyes. His hands—long fingers, sculpted nails, the hands of an artist—were her hands. No, she was hysterical, shocked beyond belief, looking for something, anything that would bind them.

'Th—thank you,' she stammered, lifting her eyes to meet his. But she didn't take the pad from him; her hand was suspended in the air.

She was shocked, yet again, because his eyes were liquid now, filled with tears. She frowned, her heart thudding heavily, and then he smiled, a little unsure.

'Yes, I think it's true,' he said gruffly. He lowered his eyes away from her, to hide his tears from her, to flick through the pad. Her watercolours of the geraniums in their terracotta pots flashed past and then Gio let out a long sigh. 'Yes, it's true,' he repeated softly.

Nina didn't understand, and nervously she found her voice. 'W-what's true?' she murmured, screwing her hands into tight fists at her sides.

He looked at her deeply and raised a dark brow. 'I think you know,' he said thickly.

And suddenly she did, and her emotions flew around her head as she wondered how this had come about. Yes, he knew who she was, and yet that couldn't be possible. *She* was the only one who knew. No one else in the whole wide world did.

'Sofia called me in the early hours and I've been here since daybreak, waiting for you.'

'Sofia?' Nina repeated faintly.

Gio's eyes met hers. Warm now, sincere. Nina held them in puzzlement.

'Sofia knew your mother. They were friends,' he told her softly. 'Last night...' He cleared his throat, uncertain, struggling. 'Sofia told me that last night the ghost of your mother walked into the room to meet her, the woman her son is going to marry.' He smiled faintly. 'Did you know you are the living, walking image of your dear mother?'

Tears now streaming down her pale face, Nina could only shake her head. A deep sob of anguish caught in her throat and then it all erupted and she was shaking with deep, racking sobs, blind with tears, and crying and crying till her heart would break.

'Dear child, dear child.' Gio gathered her into his arms and held her fiercely, his own body shaking with emotion. 'It's all right, dear child,' he whispered thickly, his voice breaking. 'Your search is over and my heart is full of happiness for us both,' he told her.

He held her tightly for a very long time, the sun beating down on their heads, the breeze soft and cooling, bringing Nina's emotions down and down till she could think more clearly.

At last Gio lifted her chin and looked down on her pale, pinched face. Smiling through his own tears, he brushed hers from her cheeks with his long artistic thumbs.

'I didn't know what to think when Lorenzo came to me with the picture he had done of you to see if I could throw any light on this Nina mystery. I couldn't help him, but the image of you he had painted disturbed me greatly. It was so like this beautiful English girl I had loved so deeply. He went on to explain how you were trying to trace me.' He shrugged slightly. 'I could think of no reason why such a beautiful young girl should have risked life and limb to come to Sicily to find me.'

'H-how could you?' Nina murmured faintly. 'You didn't know...didn't know that...I had even been born.'

He shook his head slightly. 'When I saw that picture

of you it didn't cross my mind that you were my daughter. How could it? You are right. I didn't know you had been born. I was just stunned by your resemblance to Andrea. But then Sofia called me. You were so like your mother you took her breath away.'

'But I don't understand. How could she know *anything*?'

Gio smiled. 'Come, Nina, let us walk.' He slid a comforting arm around her shoulder and together they slowly strolled along the cliff path.

'Nina,' he repeated, rolling it around his tongue as if speaking it for the very first time. 'It was the name we chose for our unborn child if it was a girl, Andrea and I, before our world was torn apart,' he mused sadly.

He smiled suddenly, as if shaking off the ghosts of the past. 'Sofia and I have no secrets from each other,' he went on. 'We go back a long way. She knew how much I loved your mother. She knew that she had written from England to say she had lost the baby and wouldn't be coming back. She knew it all and helped me over it. And now, years later, she is suddenly confronted with her son's lover who is the image of Andrea, your mother. You shocked her deeply, and then she remembered everything Lorenzo had told her about you when they got back from Milan—English girl working in Palermo, a talented artist, a few years older than Cristina and…and adopted.'

'She worked it out.' Nina laughed softly, thinking how wonderfully clever Sofia was and saying a silent prayer of thanks to Bacchus, the god of wine, for the glass of medicinal brandy that had opened up her heart and loosened her tongue to Lorenzo. Without the adoption confession no one could have linked it all.

Nina frowned suddenly, a dreadful thought crossing her mind. 'Did Sofia know I was making enquiries about you?' Had Lorenzo told his mother he had suspected her of being Gio's mistress?

Gio squeezed her shoulder and laughed. 'No, she didn't, but Lorenzo confessed to me that when he first found you he suspected we were lovers. Poor boy, he is racked with nerves over this wedding. He overreacted, knowing my fragile past. He's deeply sensitive—but you know that, of course. He's rather high-minded where affairs of the heart are concerned. He's often told me what I fool I've been—all in protection of his mother, I suppose.'

He sighed heavily and stopped on the uneven path to look at her. 'I have made mistakes, Nina, and things might have been very different if your mother and I—'

'Don't,' Nina pleaded. 'It was so sad, but fate and all that...' She sighed. 'Andrea, my mother, died...died when I was small and—'

'I know,' Gio said softly. 'When my father finally admitted that he had been responsible for breaking us up I tried to trace her, only to find she had died in a car crash. I should have dug deeper and maybe found that she had given birth to you and had you adopted.' He sighed heavily. 'How could she have done that? Didn't she know I loved her and would have looked after her?'

Nina sighed after him. 'She was young and afraid, I suppose. I gather she had no family; your father had run her out of the country and she probably felt she had no other choice. She did what she thought was best and...and I suppose we will never know anything for sure.' Nina smiled to dispel thoughts of the anguish and turmoil her mother must have suffered. 'But, Gio, this is all fate, serendipity, whatever you like to call it. You wouldn't be marrying Sofia now, who is so wonderful and has stuck by you through thick and thin, and you wouldn't have adorable Cristina, and I wouldn't have come to Sicily and found you and the man I'm going to marry—that high-minded Lorenzo Biacci who—'

'Who adores the ground you walk on,' Gio finished for her.

Nina laughed. 'I was going to say who is probably pacing up and down on the terrace this very minute, wondering where his breakfast is coming from!'

And as they slowly walked back to the house Nina told him everything that had happened since finding those papers in the bureau and making her decision to come to Sicily to find her roots. And she told him all that had happened between her and Lorenzo, and how he'd thought her a mistress and she'd gone along with it to save everyone's feelings, and how they had fallen in love, and all the turmoil of how she had loved him so much she had decided to keep her secret to ensure everyone's happiness.

And because of the way she told it, free of anxiety now, bubbling with humour, by the time they reached the house, with an exhausted Carlo dragging at their heels, they were both laughing and hugging each other.

On the terrace, Gio suddenly turned her to face him. 'Nina, my dear, have no fear that you are not a part of this extended family. Sofia has complete understanding, and last night she and Cristina talked and talked it through—Sofia telling her daughter of her suspicions. When I go inside and tell them it is true and you are my dear daughter they will be as ecstatic as I am. Cristina has always wanted a sister and now she has one, and already she adores you.'

Nina's heart nearly failed. But what about Lorenzo? It was wonderful to hear Gio's reassurances that she was welcome, but would Lorenzo share everyone else's enthusiasm? For so long she had let him believe the very worst of her. Would he ever trust her again?

She was aware of Gio hugging her warmly before leaving her on the terrace, promising her that they would talk more and fill in the multitude of gaps in their distanced lives, but she was aware of someone else, too: Lorenzo, waiting under the shade of the vines further along the terrace.

After Gio had disappeared into the house, calling out for Sofia and Cristina and gabbling in Italian, Lorenzo stepped out into brighter light, and Nina was lost and uncertain for a moment. His face was implacable, his body tense as slowly he approached her.

She backed off, suddenly so afraid, feeling her euphoria slide out of her, leaving her tense and defensive. He had seen Gio's affection, hers too. He must think...

'It isn't what you think!' she cried. 'And don't deny it! You're thinking that we are...we are...' She burst into tears again, the emotion of facing her father at last too much for her. 'He's my father!' she cried passionately. 'How could I tell you? How could I when he was about to be married? You wouldn't have believed me and—'

'Oh, my darling. I know. I know.' He reached her, pulled her into his arms and held her so fiercely her breath choked in her throat. His mouth ravaged her hair. 'I didn't before and now I do, and I love you so much for being so brave.'

'Oh, Lorenzo,' she sobbed, clawing at his hair. 'I loved you so much I didn't want to lose you. I would never have told you...I couldn't... But Sofia knew... your dear, wonderful mother knew.'

'She told me—this morning—all her suspicions, and it all fitted into place.' He breathed heatedly into her hair. 'She and Cristina have been up most of the night, waiting for Gio, knowing he would know for sure. And I've seen his face now, seen his happiness and yours.'

Nina stepped back, rubbing her face with the backs of her hands, her eyes wide and distraught. 'Oh, Lorenzo, I never wanted to upset anyone. I only found out a few weeks ago about my real father. All my life I've wanted to feel wanted. I had to find him, and then…then I found you, and it was all such a mess. But I would never have said, never admitted that Gio was my father, and now, now we all know, and though it's wonderful it's still not over. I'm happy, but sad, too, because it's too much…for everyone.'

Lorenzo gathered her into his arms once again. 'How little you know of our Sicilian ways, my darling. You are Gio's daughter, a deep, deep part of him. Of me, too, because I love you so much. And Sofia and Cristina. Did you think for one minute that we would cast you aside? You belong with us, for ever, and you will make Gio and Sofia's wedding that much more special.'

'Oh, Lorenzo,' Nina sobbed, wondering why the tears wouldn't stop when she was so happy. 'I love you so much, too. But…but you are going to have to help me, reassure me over and over again. I'm so relieved and so happy, and yet now I feel guilty over my adoptive parents. They did look after me, but they never… I do feel guilty and—'

'Shh, now, darling. If it makes you feel any better we can call them in Australia and tell them everything. Invite them to the wedding—our wedding. A Sicilian wedding because we are both home at last. They will be happy for you; I promise you they will.'

Nina clung to him, her tears dying down. 'Oh, Lorenzo, how wonderful you are. I love you more every minute.' She lifted her head back and eagerly sought his mouth to passionately show him just how deeply she felt for him.

A deep growl behind them had Lorenzo stiffening

against her. Together they turned and in unison shouted at Carlo, who glared jealously at them both from the top of the terrace steps.

'And you can cut that out!' they cried.

And as Carlo, tail between his legs, trotted up to them and slunk submissively at their feet with a whine of defeat, Lorenzo sighed and his mouth sought hers again, and when finally he drew back from her to gaze adoringly into her misty grey eyes, he murmured softly, 'I wonder if my housekeeper will agree to me keeping him?'

'You have no choice,' Nina murmured happily. 'We come as a package.'

Lorenzo grinned. 'Marry me, Nina Parker. Marry me and make me the happiest man in the world.'

Before she could utter a heartfelt yes, Carlo was on his feet. He barked three times and then slobbered all over Lorenzo's bare feet.

'There you have your answer, my wonderful, proud Sicilian lover,' Nina laughed, her eyes bright with love. 'Yes, yes, yes.'

His mouth closed over hers to seal the promise.

MILLS & BOON®

Next Month's Romances

♡

Each month you can choose from a wide variety of romance novels from Mills & Boon®. Below are the new titles to look out for next month from the Presents™ and Enchanted™ series.

Presents™

SINFUL PLEASURES	Anne Mather
THE RELUCTANT HUSBAND	Lynne Graham
THE NANNY AFFAIR	Robyn Donald
RUNAWAY FIANCÉE	Sally Wentworth
THE BRIDE'S SECRET	Helen Brooks
TEMPORARY PARENTS	Sara Wood
CONTRACT WIFE	Kay Thorpe
RED-HOT LOVER	Sarah Holland

Enchanted™

AN IDEAL WIFE	Betty Neels
DASH TO THE ALTAR	Ruth Jean Dale
JUST ANOTHER MIRACLE!	Caroline Anderson
ELOPING WITH EMMY	Liz Fielding
THE WEDDING TRAP	Eva Rutland
LAST CHANCE MARRIAGE	Rosemary Gibson
MAX'S PROPOSAL	Jane Donnelly
LONE STAR LOVIN'	Debbie Macomber

On sale from 6th April 1998

H1 9803

Available at most branches of
WH Smith, John Menzies, Martins, Tesco,
Asda, Volume One, Sainsbury and Safeway

4 FREE

books and a surprise gift!

We would like to take this opportunity to thank you for reading this Mills & Boon® book by offering you the chance to take FOUR more specially selected titles from the Presents™ series absolutely FREE! We're also making this offer to introduce you to the benefits of the Reader Service™—

- ★ FREE home delivery
- ★ FREE gifts and competitions
- ★ FREE monthly newsletter
- ★ Books available before they're in the shops
- ★ Exclusive Reader Service discounts

Accepting these FREE books and gift places you under no obligation to buy, you may cancel at any time, even after receiving your free shipment. Simply complete your details below and return the entire page to the address below. *You don't even need a stamp!*

YES! Please send me 4 free Presents books and a surprise gift. I understand that unless you hear from me, I will receive 6 superb new titles every month for just £2.30 each, postage and packing free. I am under no obligation to purchase any books and may cancel my subscription at any time. The free books and gift will be mine to keep in any case.

P8XE

Ms/Mrs/Miss/Mr ....Initials ....
BLOCK CAPITALS PLEASE

Surname ....

Address ....

....

....Postcode....................................

Send this whole page to:
THE READER SERVICE, FREEPOST, CROYDON, CR9 3WZ
(Eire readers please send coupon to: P.O. BOX 4546, DUBLIN 24.)

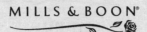

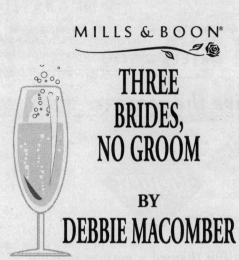

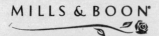
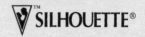